Beijing Women

Stories

Beijing Women
Stories

Wang Yuan

Translated by Colin S. Hawes
and Shuyu Kong

With an Introduction by Shuyu Kong

MerwinAsia
Portland, Maine

MERWIN

ASIA

Distributed by the University of Hawaii Press

Library of Congress Control Number: 2014931433

978-1-937385-46-0 (Paperback)
978-1-937385-47-7 (Hardcover)

Printed in the United States of America

The paper used in this publication meets the minimum
requirements of the American National Standard for
Information Services—Permanence of Paper
for Printed Library Materials, ANSI/NISO Z39/48-1992

❈ ❈ ❈
CONTENTS

v

Introduction:
Wang Yuan and Her Ethical Dramas of Everyday China
Shuyu Kong

WANG YUAN IS NOT YET A FAMOUS WRITER, BUT SHE IS one of the few writers whose fiction gives us an intimate and insightful understanding of contemporary China and its people. Behind all the high-rise apartments and glass-covered office blocks that seem to spring up overnight, the high speed trains on brand new intercity tracks, and the millions of new cars jostling for space on newly constructed freeways—behind all these symbols of a rapidly industrializing global power, how has the breakneck pace of change really had an impact on the relationships and inner emotional lives of ordinary people?

-1-

When I left China for Canada in the final weeks of 1991, I didn't realize China was on the verge of another "great transformation." In the two disheartening years after 1989, we all thought the 1980s' "golden age" of cultural enlightenment was gone forever, with many of China's brightest minds fleeing to the West to escape persecution or stagnation. I was completing my Master's in comparative literature at Peking University, and during those most oppressive days I too made the decision to move to North America to complete a Ph.D. in Asian Studies.

The world soon realized that China, far from slowing its

development, was actually intensifying the pace of its rapid march toward urbanization and commercialization. Not only would this new era vastly increase the global impact of the country from an economic, political and environmental standpoint, it would also irreversibly alter the private lives of ordinary Chinese people living through these changes. Over the next decade, in my peaceful study in Vancouver, I devoured news, gossip, letters, and e-mails from friends and relatives still in China, as if through them I could vicariously experience a life that was passing me by. Wang Yuan's stories and prose works were one of my favorite sources of information about life in China, bearing witness to her long, sometimes difficult, personal journey through the 1990s, from the leafy university campus in Beijing's northwest suburbs, overflowing with old-style humanistic idealism, to the towering office buildings, glitzy hotels and nightclubs of the Central Business District, crowded with ambitious young professionals and their staff and hangers on, pursuing careers that did not exist just a few years earlier.

Yuan was my classmate in the Chinese literature program at Peking University, but only for the final two years. She transferred over from Computer Science in 1986. Like many Chinese students, she had majored in Computer Science not so much through her own choice but to please her parents and to prove that she was bright and competitive. The Four Modernizations, Deng Xiaoping's blueprint for Chinese society, had placed science and technology at the forefront of development, and in the national university entrance exam, majors like Computer Science required better grade point averages than impractical majors like the humanities or the social sciences. Studying Computer Science would also result in a less troubled life in case another Cultural Revolution broke out. Parents' memories of that dark time when writers, artists, and intellectuals were cruelly "smashed" for their ideas and writings were still painfully fresh.

But once she reached Peking University—the most liberal and open environment in China during the 1980s—Wang Yuan gave very little attention to Computer Science and instead focused her energy mainly on reading literary works from all over the world. It was a heady time for the translation of foreign literature and philosophy, and an unprecedented smorgasbord of spiritual food became available to fascinated student readers—from Chekhov to Kafka, from Kawabata to Gabriel Garcia Marquez, from Hemingway to Kundera. Yuan immersed herself in these literary delights, and the result was that she failed most of her Computer Science subjects and happily transferred to the Department of Chinese Language and Literature.

Now she no longer needed to feel guilty spending her days and nights reading fiction. But to claim that from this point on Yuan had already decided to devote her life to writing would be an exaggeration. Like many other undergraduates facing an exciting but uncertain future, Yuan didn't really know what she wanted to do after graduation. Instead of accepting a secure state-assigned job at a cultural institute— back then still a privilege for the educated elite and the choice of most of our classmates—Yuan decided to take a risk. She parlayed her combined training in computer science and Chinese literature to land a job as a copywriter in a Sino-Japanese joint venture company. She thus became one of the first group of Chinese "white collar professionals" working at the glamorous China World Trade Center in Beijing, a landmark of China's accelerating thrust toward global capitalism.

Ironically, it was during those days of superficial glamor that Yuan first discovered the importance of writing for her personal development. She once described to me how "depressing" and "suffocating" she found the air-conditioned foreign company offices, and how the only time she felt relaxed and alive was after work when she could spend hours alone, writing. Instead of improving her Japanese or English skills, reading management or marketing texts, or registering for an MBA like most other ambitious "white collar ladies in foreign companies," she happily devoted her spare time to writing stories, finding in writing a welcome breathing space away from the claustrophobia of an office. She was further encouraged by her success in getting published in literary magazines, and she even received a writing award from *Mengya*, a literary journal for young writers in Shanghai.

Compared to her fellow graduates, in the 1990s Wang Yuan appeared to be drifting, or even swimming against the current. Years later, Wu Shihong, another "white collar lady" of the time, who had started her career on the bottom rung of IBM China as an office clerk and then taught herself English, management and human resources, and worked her way up to General Manager at Microsoft China, wrote her success into an inspirational memoir, *Flying against the Wind* (Nifeng feiyang, 1999). The memoir became one of the bestsellers of 1999–2000, inspiring a new genre of books about self-made success in China—though the genre already had a long history in the West. Alain De Bouton, in *Status Anxiety*, has ironically summarized these tomes as "autobiographies of self-made heroes [or in this case heroines] and compendia of advice directed at the not-yet-made, illustrating a morality tale of wholesale personal transformation, of the rapid attainment of vast wealth and great happiness."

Yet just as Wu Shihong was flying higher and higher over the emerging cityscape of Beijing's Central Business District and becoming a guru for a whole new generation of pushy female professionals, Wang Yuan was diving more and more deeply into the murky waters of China's brave new world. Determined to test her limits and experience a different world, she banished herself to Hainan Island—right on the wild southern edge of China, formerly known as a fearsome destination for political exiles, but since the 1990s a booming no-holds-barred business and tourist destination.

After this sojourn in Hainan, partially reflected in the story "A Slice of Ginger" (Jiangpian), came one year of graduate studies in East Asian Languages and Literatures at the University of Oregon. But Yuan found she wasn't so much a wandering academic as a drifter, and she soon returned to Beijing to try a brand new venture: opening her own restaurant. Yes, it was noisy and polluted back in Beijing, unlike the clear air and peaceful surroundings of Eugene, but life in China was so full of stories!

Yuan's business venture would prove as short-lived as all the other careers she had already tried, and in the mid-2000s she went overseas again, this time for the education of her two young children, residing in a succession of foreign countries—New Zealand, Canada, the United States—restlessly seeking a better life for the children like so many Chinese immigrants on the road. At the time of writing, she is back in Beijing once more: a drifting kite whose sting is tied to a place she can never really escape.

Throughout these years of change, writing has been the only "career" that Yuan has really persisted with. Whatever one may feel about her rootless life, it has certainly provided fertile material for her creative work. In China, she has published four novels, one collection of lyrical prose works, and one collection of short stories: *Kouhong* (Lipstick), from which the translations in this book are selected. Two of the stories in the collection, including the title story, were short-listed for the prestigious Lu Xun Literary Awards. Through the art of writing, the scenes that she encountered in her variegated experiences of the 1990s and 2000s are crystalized into poignant and unforgettable human dramas.

-2-

The stories in *Beijing Women* delineate the drama of mobility, aspiration, separation and the "all that is solid melts into air" existence of ordinary people in a rapidly changing urban China, "from a unique woman's point of view," in the words of feminist cultural critic Dai Jinhua. In these quiet yet clear-eyed observations of women's fragility, calculation, resilience, and career and emotional struggles, Wang reminds us of the constant ethical and spiritual dilemmas that confront the Chinese people in a dramatically transforming society. Though not suffused with outrage or emotional bluster, in their ironic and psychologically astute portraits of female and male characters, Yuan's stories reveal far more subtle and complex critiques of power, capital, and gender inequality than many so-called feminist Chinese writers.

In his review of John Cheever's 1943 collection *The Way Some People Live*, the American writer Struthers Burt celebrates Cheever's "sense of drama in ordinary events and people": "the underlying and universal importance of the outwardly unimportant; a deep feeling for the perversities and contradictions, the worth and unexpected dignity of life, its ironies, comedies, and tragedies." In many ways, Wang Yuan provides a Chinese counterpart to Cheever's exploration of the everyday psychological drama of American life. The four stories collected here encapsulate those everyday moments when individuals, uncontrollably swept along or obstructed by the evolving environment around them, become vulnerable and sensitized to individual ruptures and interpersonal conflicts.

In "Lipstick," the drama is generated from the misperceptions of the three characters about each other, and the resulting tensions and conflicts: Xiao, the taxi driver, is in many ways typical of the urban "working class," struggling to make ends meet and failing to benefit from the government's economic reforms and "opening up" policies. Partly because of his present failures, he stubbornly clings to an old-fashioned socialist moralism which justifies his venting his resentment toward the nouveau riche and other "sorts" engaged in shady business. This resentment is heightened by his frustration with his exploitative manager, who refuses to provide him with a replacement car so he can get his taxi repaired. He is forced to continue driving his taxi without air-conditioning in Beijing's uncomfortably hot summer. This is the cue for a young female customer, Chen, to hire Xiao's taxi. Seeing her flashy clothes and dyed red hair, Xiao immediately jumps to the conclusion that Chen is "that sort of woman," and he decides to act as a self-appointed moral guardian determined to catch her in the act and expose her.

For her part, Chen, a struggling but ambitious singer willing to do anything to advance her singing career, is equally contemptuous toward Xiao, whom she views as a typical loser. What really annoys her is Xiao's insinuations about her moral character, possibly because he has hit a sensitive spot. After all, she is on her way to meet a visiting Hong Kong music producer at his hotel in the late evening.

The tension and mutual revulsion between Chen and Xiao—symbolized by the scarlet smear of lipstick on Chen's face caused by the driver's deliberate sudden swerve—are observed by Shen, a fellow passenger in the taxi and the third person in this drama. A professionally trained manager working in a hotel near Beijing Airport that has many foreign guests, Shen sees herself as superior in every sense to the other two characters. At first she is just an onlooker watching the sparks fly between the other two. But Xiao's suspicions about Chen start to worry her, not just because the Hong Kong producer whom Chen is meeting is a guest at her hotel, but more crucially because this producer could be highly useful to her own brother, another struggling singer hoping to be "discovered" and to escape from grubby obscurity. As a result, Shen cannot remain a neutral observer but must wrestle with her own moral conflicts as she tries to sort out the dispute between the two warring characters, while at the same time promoting her brother's interests.

The story ends in tragedy, but the true sadness lies in the misunderstandings, mutual suspicion, and revulsion among these ordinary characters, who are all really in the same boat, struggling to escape the frustrations that life throws at them. As Xiao the taxi driver puts it: "She was a kind of person similar to him, yet she still wanted to cheat him. When you linked her up together with everyone else, they formed this immense gray force arrayed against him. And who were all these other people? . . . Xiao couldn't put his finger on it. He just felt he was stuck in a gray world, a world he couldn't describe clearly but which went to enormous lengths to make life difficult for him. Xiao did his best to fight back against that world, but right now he couldn't even work out where he should aim his blows."

"Lipstick" exemplifies Yuan's distinctive style: her careful observation of character and subtle sense of compassion which reveals the fallacies as well as the vulnerabilities of human beings. While she can be sharply ironic in portraying peoples' vanity and greed, she also understands their desperation and pitiful weakness, and she depicts these same characters engaging in tender moments of reflection, such as in this passage describing Chen at the end of "Lipstick": "Suddenly the thought came to her, *If she simply worked steadily, adding one brick and one tile at a time, wouldn't she find her success in the end?* But then she also thought: *No, when it comes down to it, people are not bricks and tiles. They're a lot weaker and more fragile. Bricks and tiles can wait a hundred years or a thousand years, but people just don't have time to hang around, following the prescribed order* . . . Chen Xiaohong kept looking toward those towering skyscrapers glistening like fish scales, pushing past her like surging wind-blown clouds. She felt sad, but also proud, and this powerful mix of emotions inexorably overflowed into tears running down her face."

Chen Xiaohong's reflections on the short-cut mentality of ambitious young Chinese chasing their dreams sheds some light on the behavior of the characters in "Deception" (Qipian), a psychological drama that focuses on one young soul lost in a morally confusing world, detailing the subtle progression of her loss of innocence over one summer break.

On the surface, Lin Duoduo's life could not be more different from that of Chen Xiaohong. A senior majoring in English at an elite university, Lin and her classmates have a much brighter future than most of their contemporaries: they can choose either to go abroad for graduate studies or to find a good-paying job in a foreign-invested company. But precisely because of the deceptive proximity between their dreams and their present reality as poor college students, the temptations of taking a short cut seem even harder to resist. For her classmates, such as Du Juan, who are determined to study abroad, the temptation is to forge their transcripts without being discovered; for Duoduo, the temptation is to earn easy money by fraudulently sitting exams for other people! The story thus revolves around these two parallel events, which seem to exemplify the meaning of deception, one at the individual level and the other at the collective level.

For non-Chinese who have read news reports about the forged transcripts and TOEFL/GRE/SAT scores of Chinese students, the puzzling and disturbing question is why this obvious moral failure occurs among these bright young people who should already have all the resources to realize their dreams. "Deception" gives us an insider's glimpse into the moral abyss that Chinese society has become and into that which no one can resist being sucked into until their sense of direction is lost without a trace. Obviously, in this story the problem is the failure of the Chinese education system. Far from forming new socialist citizens, free from egotistical greed, commodity fetishism and capitalist morality, the system has instead created isolated, cynical individualists who are skilled at double talk and taking advantage of the loopholes in society. This cynicism and hypocrisy is best embodied by Li Hao, the confident young lecturer who is progressing very well with his career but seems to lack any real feelings, let alone guilt, about his immoral sexual fling with his student Duoduo. With such an insensitive and morally suspect teacher preaching at them from on high, it is not surprising that the students work together behind the scenes to cheat the system, with their fake university seals "inherited" from previous students, under the leadership of their "class representative" Du Juan. Nobody seems to worry about whether what they are doing is right or wrong but only whether they might be caught—in fact the reader may be stunned by the childish and innocent manner in which they forge their transcripts. In a society where material success has become the be-all and end-all, people can be so "open-minded" and "carefree" about moral issues!

The "faceless" woman Xu Yawen, whose identity Lin Duoduo borrows for her own adventure, is the ultimate representative of this impetuous, pragmatic, yet amoral crowd. Xu is so desperate to go abroad that she tries all imaginable methods: applying to obscure colleges; immigrating to any country that will take her; finding an online "husband." The ethical implications never seem to cross her mind. Clearly Ms. Xu, who Duoduo and the reader never meet in person, is just one of many customers of the agent Wan's prosperous business, and it is surely no accident that her surname, especially when pronounced by the foreigner Robert, sounds the same as "empty," "fake" or "non-existent" (*xu*) in Chinese. In a moment of weakness and loneliness, struggling with betrayal by the two-faced Li Hao, Lin Duoduo adopts Xu's identity and starts her free fall: first she sits an English exam for Xu, and then (still pretending to be Xu) she accepts an invitation to have a fling with a visitor from the U.S. Perhaps she is seeking some kind of reckless revenge on Li Hao, or just trying to overcome her despair through self-abandonment.

What makes this story even more poignant is the fact that in her struggle against losing her self-identity, there seems to be no one Duoduo can trust to share her dark secrets with.

She is well aware that Du Juan's apparent concern is just a search for incriminating information that Du Juan can use to control Duoduo and prevent her from exposing their forgery operation. And the popular teacher Li Hao is the very reason for her despair. So Duoduo must put on a brave and cynical face to those "friends" or "teachers" who interrogate her, not just because they are no better than she, but because telling the truth will reveal that her whole life has become a lie.

Thus, after completely transforming herself into another person, a virtual person she imagines living in the rich and glorious world of Beijing's most exclusive apartment district, Duoduo's inner (true) self can only emerge in her subconscious, taking her back to where she originally comes from: "In her dreams, she always seemed to be running too slowly. In her dreams she was an eraser, flying back in time, rubbing out everything that had happened in her life. All the places she had ever visited were sketched on a crumpled piece of paper . . . the drawings of all those places were rubbed out leaving no traces. But each time she rubbed something out, she lost a part of herself, too, because she was the eraser . . . The longest and most difficult part of her dream was when she reached Beijing Station and took a train all the way south, finally arriving at a fairytale scene of clear mountains, pure waters, and luxuriant forests. In her dream she told herself: *This is the end of the paper scroll; you won't ever come this far again. Your grimy body has already been reduced to countless tiny flakes of rubber. If you go any further, nothing will be left of you.* But why was she so reluctant to wake up even now? It's because just then, on the horizon, she saw the beautiful, pure light of a new dawn of innocence." This ending evokes in me the same kind of sadness and disturbance as David Lynch's *Mulholland Drive*, with its once innocent and bright-eyed character who has dreamed herself into a nightmare in which she is forever trapped.

"A Slice of Ginger" continues Wang Yuan's exploration of the subtle and complex interpersonal relationships in a society where egalitarian socialism is being uprooted and replaced by dog-eat-dog capitalism. Yuan is particularly convincing when she depicts the dilemmas faced by urban women in a newly commoditized society—in this case, Beijing women trying to make their way in a South China economic zone. The drama in "A Slice of Ginger" unfolds around the psychological maneuvering among a small group of characters, a microcosm of the opportunist calculations, capital exchanges, class conflicts and power struggles that are a constant feature of the broader Chinese society. The narrator "I" (Linda) is a PR woman—a very elastic job description in China. She has moved from Beijing to work for a company on Hainan Island, notorious for its illicit sex trade and for being a wild frontier where quick-thinking people can get rich in an instant. During one eventful evening, she encounters the harsh reality of the business world, where power, sex and money are inextricably linked and PR women may be required not only to drink on behalf of their boss to please potential "customers" but even to provide more intimate "companionship" for key clients—in this case for Mr. Chen, the "Oil King." While Linda understands perfectly what her boss Guan wants her to do, she feels insulted by the naked truth that she is being offered in a business deal. She decides that Mr. Chen, a skinny, short and small-minded man with nothing but money to recommend himself, is only worth a local "escort" at the night club (Lucy).

In this contest of male pride, manipulation and control,

beauty and youth become a form of hard currency and a rare commodity. Wang Yuan shows how Chinese women have to learn to survive in a male-dominated, commercialized society, using their "capital resources" to advance their own interests and defend themselves, as Linda manages to do. Yet unlike some female writers, who seem to believe all social problems are caused by inborn conflicts between the two sexes, Wang Yuan understands that gender relations are only part of the more complex human interaction within each specific environment, and the situation in her stories is never clear-cut or easy to analyze based on gender stereotypes. While it is true that "A Slice of Ginger" depicts an opportunistic male-dominated environment in which "money is everything" and women can be "sacrificed" in the male competition for wealth and power, Wang also recognizes the complex humanity of some of her male characters too. Linda's boss Mr. Guan, for example, while ready to "offer up" Linda to cement his deal with Mr. Chen, feels occasional pangs of guilt, and motivated partly by pride and partly by the lingering residue of his moral conscience, ultimately decides to walk away from the deal.

In a further complexity, the women in Wang's stories are not averse to using other women to achieve their self-interested aims too. Linda "uses" Lucy the escort to relieve her of the burden of entertaining Mr. Chen, and Linda's convoluted self-justification for this course of action provides one of the more ironic episodes of the story: "I felt a bit guilty again about Lucy. The guilt weighed down on my head like a heavy burden. But I wasn't someone who easily admitted my mistakes, even when I was arguing with my own conscience. I started justifying myself: I hadn't forced her to do anything; whatever she did was her own free will. And don't forget, this is her job, so if I introduce her to a client, I'm actually helping her out, aren't I?"

But in fact Lucy has her own ways of protecting herself, such as constantly snacking on preserved ginger so men have no chance to kiss her, and eventually Linda realizes that Lucy knows better than most how to survive in this shady environment.

The story thus captures the subtle, slippery and often tricky relationships, dilemmas and obstacles facing young women in today's China. Wang Yuan's description of Linda's drunkenness is symptomatic of the pervasive social disparity and instability that seems to cause everybody to tumble off their moral perches: "Looking back on that night, I can still feel exactly what it was like. It was as if everything around me was getting in my way: whenever I tried to move forward, a massive force seemed to block me; but when I tried to stand still, another massive force suddenly unblocked me and pushed me from behind until I fell over."

The sophisticated ironic rhetoric in stories such as "A Slice of Ginger" is a quality rarely found in contemporary Chinese fiction, which often seems too clear-cut in its moralistic didacticism to capture the many shades of human complexity. On one level, we see through the narrator Linda's eyes that the conceited nouveau riche Mr. Chen either doesn't know or refuses to admit his pitiful failure at attracting women. On another level, the ironic spotlight is re-directed toward Linda herself, as her sense of moral superiority and simplistic misunderstanding of the other characters is undermined by Mr. Guan's bitter remarks about Beijing women and by Lucy's unexpected revelation to her at the end. This "disparity between the facts of a situation and the character's understanding of it," in David Lodge's words, is typical of "dramatic irony." In the case of Wang Yuan's works, it has its source in the social stratification and isolation caused by rapid economic development, and the flailing attempts by people to make sense of their new identities and their changed relationships, with little but their own flawed instincts to guide them.

The social relevance of this dramatic irony becomes most evident in the final story, "Beijing Woman" (Beijing ren). Although all the stories in this collection focus primarily on women, the title Beijing ren in Chinese can actually refer to both men and women, and it has rich associations and ironic undertones. First of all, Beijing ren inevitably evokes images of Peking Man, the earliest specimen of Chinese humanoid excavated at Zhoukoudian, a suburb of modern-day Beijing, which suggests that the story is itself a kind of anthropological dissection of universal human behavior. Second, it also reminds readers of a play with the same title by the famous modern dramatist Cao Yu (1910–1996), a masterpiece from the early twentieth century portraying a scholar-official family in decline and their poignant relationships at the dawn of modern China. In Wang Yuan's work we see a new kind of human drama set at the turn of the new millennium. Third, the title may point to the collaborative oral history project initiated in the 1980s by the Chinese writers and social historians Zhang Xinxin and Sang Ye, from which a series of a hundred or so interviews were published in a book called Beijing ren in 1986.[1] And certainly the focus on ordinary people going about their lives as best they can is an

1. The abridged English translation of Zhang and Sang's work is titled Chinese Lives: An Oral History of Contemporary China (1987).

important aspect of Wang's work too.

Yet most Chinese readers seeing this title would think first
of Beijing people as a regional group enjoying privileges and
opportunities bestowed on them by virtue of living in the
capital city, close to the central government; people who have
an inborn sense of superiority as the most cultivated and best
educated citizens in China; people who often look down on
those who come from other regions of the country. Anyone
who has lived in China will have encountered the impact of
this kind of regional prejudice, a whole set of stereotypes
based on the particular dialect or accent with which someone
speaks. For example, Shanghai people are often associated
with cosmopolitanism and sophistication, but at the same
time they are despised by people from other regions for their
snobbery, foreign-worship and stinginess. Henan people
evoke images of poverty and rural migrants, frequently
blamed for rising crime levels in the city. Wenzhou people
are known for their shrewd business sense, especially in
overseas markets, but they are also demonized for producing
fake or poor quality goods that damage China's international
reputation and cause consumer scandals at home.

Wang Yuan's "Beijing Woman" focuses on the "pride and
prejudice" of a woman from Beijing as she interacts with other
Beijingers and with migrant workers who have swarmed into
Beijing from all over China. Like the other female characters
in this collection, Lin Baihui, a former school teacher turned
restaurant owner, seems to veer between overconfidence and
confusion in running her business venture and sorting out
her relationships. She is forced to seek a new identity and
equilibrium in a society that is dramatically changing, where
past experience and moral beliefs have become irrelevant.
Not only must she deal with various bureaucratic government

officials, from the Small Business Bureau to the police and the local neighborhood committee, who are constantly harassing her for money; she must also try to manage and train a feisty group of employees, mostly teenage girls from the countryside, who seem to have little idea how to behave, and talk, in the big city environment.

While this "floating population" of rural migrant workers has become essential for the cost-effective operation of her business, Lin Baihui, like most Beijing people, doesn't think much of them. She often has an uncontrollable urge to "civilize" them—the most obvious example being her tendency to correct their rural dialects. She claims this is not the prejudice of a Beijing resident: she says she is teaching them "Standard Chinese," not "Beijing Chinese." But her employees see through her pretense and also often question her business management skills. Her manager, a clever Sichuan lad, suggests that the only reason Lin can successfully operate her business is because she is a Beijing woman, and this gives her immunity from most of the systemic discrimination faced by migrant workers: "In the past, he had tried running his own restaurant and failed, but instead of learning from the experience, he liked to blame his failure on the fact that he wasn't from Beijing."

The rigid Chinese social structure is not only manifested in linguistic and cultural terms, but has also had a major effect on peoples' mental state and material existence. A key focus of the story is the impact of having a Beijing household registration (*hukou*), which the vast majority of people can only obtain through inheritance from their parents or through marriage. For more than half a century, the *hukou* system in China has segregated rural and urban populations and acted as a highly effective, but deeply unfair, method of governance and social control. Along with its physical restrictions, it has had a deep impact on Chinese peoples' psyche and human relationships. This impact has become increasingly evident since the reform period, when much of the rural population has flooded into cities to look for jobs that city people are not willing to do. Rather than allowing these migrant workers to settle permanently in cities, which would create a major burden on urban social services, the government has for the last three decades imposed a system which requires every migrant worker to register for a temporary residence permit in the city where they work with the assistance of their urban employer. This system obviously gives a great deal of control to employers, and they in turn have often used the promise of a residence permit to exploit their migrant workers.

In "Beijing Woman," Lin Baihui's character, and especially her air of superiority and entitlement compared to her employees, must be understood within this social context. The power of the temporary residence permit provides the excuse for Lin to disguise her shabby conduct toward employees, to go back on her promises, and to exchange favors with a local government official at the expense of a young migrant girl's mental health. But it also means that migrant workers like Xingli, her sister Erli, and their father must accept and rationalize the harsh working conditions and blatant exploitation by their employers, because that is the only way for them to satisfy the requirements for staying in Beijing. And at least in Beijing they can earn some kind of living, unlike in their rural villages where there are no jobs and abject poverty abounds.

There is nothing much that the characters can do to challenge the government's unfair household registration system, so Xingli and her family are in a particularly vulnerable situation. They never even dare to confront Lin directly for her shabby treatment of Erli. But at the end of the story, Lin herself notices something different in Xingli's eyes, possibly a reflection of her own subconscious disturbed by her heartless action: "Xingli's look gave Lin Baihui a major shock. What did she mean by this look? Having stopped reflecting on things a long time ago, Lin Baihui had now become a simple-minded person; it seemed she no longer had the linguistic ability to explain the shock that Xingli's look had given her. All she knew was that it made her feel uncomfortable. That look penetrated the fog that had been shrouding her eyes for such a long time and pierced her right in the heart."

In these four stories, Wang Yuan patiently directs our attention to the contradictions of all human beings: their fallacies and moral struggles, their fragility and resilience, their resourcefulness and occasional cruelty. She reminds us that their faults are partly caused by an unfair political system and uneven economic development, but also partly by universal human traits like greed and vanity. In the manner of all great writers, she does this with skill, irony, and quiet yet precise observation. Reading her works, one comes to understand Chinese people in a whole new complex light.

Beijing Women
Stories

LIPSTICK

THE TAXI DISPATCHER SAT IN THE CONTROL ROOM transmitting the five PM weather forecast: "The Beijing weather network tells us it will be a clear night, with wind gusting to two or three knots, probability of precipitation thirty percent and a minimum temperature of twenty degrees Celsius . . ." He suddenly felt a cool breeze blowing on his neck, and turning to look outside, he saw a persistent drizzle falling. *You call that a forecast!?* he thought to himself, and cursed. He decided to improvise. "And by mid-evening the probability of light rain will rise to one hundred percent!" Then he laughed and clicked off the microphone.

Everyone heard his laughter reverberating around the office block and throughout the huge taxi lot. Xiao Jianguo and his boss, both sitting in the manager's office, couldn't help laughing too, and that helped to relieve the tension slightly. Xiao Jianguo had been sitting there for quite a while. He drove one of the company's Xiali compacts, and the air conditioning system had failed yet again right in the middle of Beijing's fierce summer. After two days of sweltering, he'd returned to the company to demand they fix it. "Of course it can be fixed: just leave it in the repair shop and pick it up in a couple of days," said his boss."Can't you give me a replacement, otherwise what am I supposed to do for the

1

next two days?" "You're lucky to get it repaired at all. You won't find this kind of service anywhere else," the manager retorted. "Other companies are more likely to brush you off or charge you a monthly repair fee. You should be grateful for small mercies!" "Of course I know all about the company benefits, otherwise I'd soon be tempted by all those other firms with lower monthly fees. But boss, just think, it's the hottest time of the year, and anyone who can't stand the heat is going to choose a Xiali taxi because they know it has AC. If I take a two-day break, think how much money we'll lose!"

His boss remained unmoved. He'd obviously made his best offer. Xiao Jianguo was still sitting there stubbornly when the loudspeaker broadcast the dispatcher's last words: "By mid-evening the probability of light rain will rise to a hundred percent . . . Hehehe! Hehe!"

Immediately the manager's expression changed, "Look, it's raining. Maybe that will bring down the temperature." Xiao Jianguo knew he was wasting his time sitting there glaring at his boss, who obviously wanted to leave for the night. So he reluctantly stood up and headed out. His boss accompanied him to the door, patting him on the shoulder, saying, "You know, Xiao, if it's too hot in the daytime you can always do the night shift. It's cooler at night." Xiao Jianguo said nothing, but just as he got to the door, his boss suddenly added: "AC's not so great anyway. Did you hear about that driver last week? He was waiting for someone at the airport and left his air conditioner on all night. After a while he fell asleep and suffocated in his car."

Now that was news to Xiao Jianguo. He had already gone out the door, but he couldn't help turning to ask: "Why was that?" The manager shrugged and replied: "Laws of nature, I guess. I don't know. Stale air or something. Just be aware that these things can happen: I'm not just inventing stories to stop you complaining!"

Xiao Jianguo felt really frustrated, but what could he do? He would have to put off the repairs for now—he couldn't afford to lose the fares. But he just didn't understand it. True, two wasted days would be a big loss for him, but wouldn't it be an equally big loss for the company? Why didn't his boss just think for a minute? Was the air conditioning being fixed for Xiao Jianguo's benefit alone? He didn't get it. Why do some people seem to love screwing things up—not just screwing other people but screwing themselves too?

Full of resentment, Xiao Jianguo walked along the dark corridor, bumping past several office staff returning from the canteen. Xiao Jianguo completely ignored them and just carried on walking straight ahead. He never liked those people at the best of times. In his opinion, drivers like him worked themselves to death to support parasites like that. They ignored him too; they all disliked him for his volatile temper. Of course, everyone has a temper, that was forgivable. But one's temper should be matched by one's position in life. Xiao Jianguo was already a driver, a pretty good job, but he still had such a bad temper: this was something they couldn't comprehend or forgive. That's why Xiao Jianguo never got much assistance from the office staff.

Xiao Jianguo emerged from the main door and stood in the porch looking at the falling rain. He didn't have an umbrella, but the rain wasn't heavy, so he decided to just walk through it to the parking lot. He was about to step out into the rain when someone caught his eye: the young dispatcher, wearing a bright yellow tracksuit. He had just finished his dispatches and was coming back leaping over the puddles.

This dispatcher was actually a high school graduate who had only recently got the job, and despite the fact that Xiao Jianguo hated everyone else in the company, for some reason he kind of liked this kid. He smiled and greeted him: "Hey Li, your forecast was pretty accurate eh!" Li laughed as he had done before, but almost before he finished laughing the cool rain suddenly stopped. "Hell's teeth!" Xiao Jianguo cursed, then stepped off the porch. His head was hunched into his shoulders as if he still expected to get soaked with rain.

By six o'clock, the evening sun was shining on the rain-wet streets.

Chen Xiaohong stood under the Dabeiyao Bridge trying to hail a cab. She was wearing a new skirt she had just bought at the World Trade Mall. With one hand she held up the skirt hem to avoid it being splashed by passing cars and with the other she signaled for a taxi. She was heading for the Capital Guesthouse near Xiaotianzhu. Though it was just two or three kilometers from the airport, most taxi drivers didn't like to go there and waste those awkward two or three kilometers. Of course there were some who were happy to go there for a hundred yuan, non-negotiable, that being their lowest offer. As she stood in the flow of traffic, Chen Xiaohong made a quick calculation and worked out that her destination was at most twenty-five kilometers away, so she gritted her teeth and stopped a Xiali cab.

Just as she said "Capital Guesthouse" to the driver, another woman appeared beside her who also wanted to go there. It must have been her lucky day! Chen Xiaohong looked at her delightedly, and the other woman also seemed pretty happy—they felt like battle comrades encountering each other deep in enemy territory. They immediately agreed to share the taxi and split the fare evenly. Chen Xiaohong sat in the passenger seat by the driver, and the other woman sat in the back. The only one who wasn't happy was the driver, Xiao Jianguo. Of course he didn't lose anything from this deal, but he was already in a foul mood, and he resented these two women getting such a bargain. As he stuck his head out the window to drive off, he purposely tried to put a fly in their ointment: "If you're paying together, who am I supposed to give the receipt to?"

Both Chen Xiaohong and the woman said they didn't need a receipt.

Xiao Jianguo then had nothing to complain about so he got the car moving. The red Xiali pulled away from the curb and into the flow of traffic, which was barely crawling forward. It was smack in the middle of the evening rush hour, and the cars were bumper-to-bumper all the way from Dabeiyao to the Jingguang Towers.

"Which route should we take?" Xiao Jianguo asked. "The third ring road is sure to be completely tied up at this time of day." "Which way? You're asking me which way?" Chen Xiaohong snapped. "Why don't you just take a detour out past the Great Wall and back through Inner Mongolia!" Chen Xiaohong was one of those people who liked to make a clear distinction between hiring and being hired. When she was hired to work for someone else, *she* certainly wouldn't keep picking holes in what she was told to do. Likewise, when she was the one doing the hiring, she couldn't stand it when the person under her made a fuss. She considered this to be proper professional behavior, and she was pained that so few taxi drivers seemed to grasp the concept. *If I tell you to go somewhere, you should just go. Everyone knows*

5

there is a traffic jam, but if I still take a taxi in the middle of a jam, it's because I have no other choice. Of course at *midnight there wouldn't be any traffic, but who goes to the Capital Guesthouse at midnight? You should be happy to get the fare. Why waste your energy with all this empty talk?* If she had been in a bad mood, she would have recited this whole speech out loud. But today she was feeling pretty good. So she allowed her silence to express her contempt. Still, Xiao Jianguo was able to divine her unspoken thoughts. Taxi drivers deal with people every day, and they encounter every variety of human expression. There may be thousands of different faces, but you could boil them all down to a few personality types, in Xiao's opinion. Chen Xiaohong was obviously the kind of person who once she gets a bit of money instantly thinks she's the bee's knees. But take a look at her and you wonder where that money came from exactly. Xiao Jianguo gave her a sidelong glance, reflecting her unspoken contempt right back in her face.

Chen Xiaohong felt the anger rising up inside her. *Doesn't this guy know when to stop?* She decided to set his priorities straight. "Look, driver, what a sweet job you have here. You can make fifty or sixty yuan in one trip!" Xiao Jianguo immediately snapped back, "You call that sweet? I'll get nothing on the way back and I'll have wasted over twenty kilometers." Chen Xiaohong persisted: "You could go and hole up at the airport, and wait for a night flight to come in, then you'll be able to rip some poor sucker off no problem!" "I knew it from the start, Miss: you are more wicked than I am!"

While they bickered back and forth like this, the taxi was hardly moving. Chen Xiaohong finally realized how bad the traffic really was and she couldn't help feeling agitated.

She began shifting from side to side nervously, and the faux dignified air she had adopted since getting into the taxi vanished. In fact, most of that dignified air was due to her new clothes, but it was clear that the clothes didn't make the woman anymore. Xiao Jianguo's sneer grew even wider, and Chen Xiaohong kept nagging away at him and shouting, "Move it man, catch up with that guy!" Her voice had a distinctive tone, jarring the ears and leaving one feeling rather uncomfortable.

Up to now the woman sitting behind them hadn't said a word, but now she passed forward a CD and asked: "Driver, is your stereo working?" Xiao Jianguo took the disk and inserted it. The sound of soft rock filled the car.

With the music playing, Chen Xiaohong grew silent for a while. But the numbers on the meter were increasing as if by magic, even though the taxi hadn't even crossed the World Trade Center overpass. Chen Xiaohong decided to raise some more hell. A car drove past them squeezing along the bicycle lane, so Chen Xiaohong pointed at its disappearing form and asked: "Why don't you take a leaf out of his book?"

Xiao Jianguo gave a sniff, "He's breaking the law," he said. Chen Xiaohong adopted a softer more conciliatory tone: "If you go faster you'll be able to get more customers won't you, driver?" "What happens if I bump into the police and get fined?" "Go on, take a chance. If you're stopped by the police you'll get a ten yuan fine, and if you're not stopped, you could earn a hundred more in the time you save."

"Earn a hundred yuan? Miss, I don't earn money as easily as you do!" Xiao Jianguo shot back.

"I earn money easily? What's that supposed to mean?" Xiao Jianguo's insinuation didn't just shock Chen Xiaohong, it also gave the woman in the back seat a bit of a jolt. She took a good long look at Chen Xiaohong's back. From that angle, there didn't appear to be anything untoward about her, except of course for her dyed red hair.

Shen Ruolang was the night manager in the Guest Services Department at the Capital Guesthouse. Earlier she had been standing under the China World Trade Center Bridge, planning to catch the 403 Bus to work. But she was a little later than usual. Worried she wouldn't make it in time for the change of shift, she was debating whether it would be too extravagant to take a taxi instead. Just then she overheard Chen Xiaohong's shrill voice on her right, "to the Capital Guesthouse." In a flash, Shen Ruolang went over to join her. Her only thought had been to save half the taxi fare; she hadn't bothered to check what kind of person Chen Xiaohong was and why she wanted to get to the "Capital." But now, with nothing else to do, she started to pay more attention to the girl's appearance.

Working every day in the hotel, Shen Ruolang had developed a method for evaluating people, which she called "labeling." She was convinced she could judge people's status and position based upon the subtle features of their outward appearance. Labeling was an abstract concept that included peoples' clothing, make-up, accents, and so on. No single factor was decisive, but the most important component was outward appearance, otherwise how could it be called a "label"? Shen Ruolang probably wouldn't have considered her method totally scientific, but in the hotel business science wasn't required, as long as you don't make any serious errors of judgment. On top of that, she had to meet so many people every day. If she stopped to make a rigorous analysis of each one before deciding how to deal with them, it would seriously lower her efficiency level.

When Shen Ruolang had first started working she'd always worried that she would misjudge someone. She had imbibed countless moral tales from the old days in which people would make their first appearance in the shabbiest rags, but after receiving scornful treatment at the hands of a snob, they would then reveal their true exalted status, making that snob feel thoroughly ashamed and forcing her to suddenly turn polite and offer them the best seats in the house. But having worked for many years now, she realized those kinds of people with so much time on their hands were a thing of the past. These days everyone preferred to focus on efficiency, not just Shen Ruolang herself but the guests too. And because guests generally found that those in Shen Ruolang's position tended to use labeling methods to evaluate others, they would make a special effort to attach obvious labels to themselves, and both sides would work together to make the labeling method more and more effective.

Here was another case in point, Shen Ruolang thought triumphantly. Chen Xiaohong's red dyed hair immediately marked her as "that sort of woman." But even though Shen Ruolang had now established this without a shred of doubt in her mind, she didn't feel the need to discriminate against her. Having worked for so long in a hotel, Shen Ruolang treated every kind of person first and foremost as a potential guest. All the more so since this particular "guest" was willing to go halves with her for a taxi. Therefore, out of the goodness of her own heart, she decided to save Chen Xiaohong from embarrassment, so she asked the two people in front, "So what do you think of the music?"

"It's good stuff!" each of them announced. Hearing this, Shen Ruolang couldn't help feeling happy for her younger brother. The reason she was late for work was that just now she had picked up this demo recording from her brother. Shen Ruolang herself grew up in an ordinary working class household, but through hard work and determination, she managed to complete her education, get a white-collar job, and enjoy some of the perks of a middle class life. She had focused all her energies on practical things like learning foreign languages, and she had no time or money to waste on artistic pursuits. But by the time her brother went to school, because she was able to support him a bit, he could indulge his weakness for music. So now the challenge that most occupied her was how to guide and support his career. Shen Ruolang often thought it a pity that a bright boy like him didn't study accounting, management, or business administration—that would give him much better prospects. But her efforts to persuade him were in vain. And since she didn't know the first thing about music and couldn't discuss it intelligently with him, she had no idea whether his songs were any good. This was why, everywhere she went, she sought out other peoples' opinions, and was especially happy to hear them praise his music.

As for Xiao Jianguo, he really did think this song was pretty good, and since he listened to 97.4 FM on the car stereo when he had time, his music appreciation abilities were at least more reliable than Shen Ruolang's. Thinking that it was good, he then wanted to find out the name of the song, so he stopped the disk, pulled it out, and had a look. But there was no label on it.

"This is a little demo album that my brother created; it hasn't actually been produced by a record label yet," Shen Ruolang explained.

Chen Xiaohong was amazed by this and turning to her, said, "Is your brother a musician? What kind of music:

classical or popular?"

Shen Ruolang responded, "I'm not sure myself. But I do know he has lots of friends who are also musicians." Having said this, she sensed the taxi driver snorting derisively, and she thought to herself: *Probably this driver thinks I'm just a con artist or something.* So she didn't say anything else. Indeed, Xiao Jianguo was thinking exactly that. Apart from his strong dislike for the nouveau riche, another class of people he disdained were those who claimed to "understand the arts." What kind of art would it be if anyone could understand it? Only a couple of days ago, someone had set up a date for him with a girl who claimed to be a "lover of photography," but who was actually just a lover of "making silly poses and preening in front of the camera." That really spoiled his date. And now here we had a so-called "music lover." What a bunch of freaks he had sitting in his car: obviously it just wasn't his day!

Still, this music wasn't half bad. As he kept listening he couldn't help nodding his head and praising it. "Not bad at all, pretty sophisticated stuff." Curious, Shen Ruolang asked, "So driver, do you also understand music?" "Sure do. Started learning piano when I was small, and almost passed the entrance exam for the Music Academy Middle School. But with my family's class background, they failed me for political reasons."

Looking at Xiao Jianguo's back, Shen Ruolang felt he was a bit too young for that. He didn't seem to belong to the generation who were held back when their parents were accused of being rightists. People like that would have to be at least forty by now. But this guy was only thirty, tops. These days, someone in his thirties who was a failure had only himself to blame. Shen Ruolang gave a sniff —it was her turn to treat Xiao Jianguo as a con artist.

Chen Xiaohong wasn't as profound a thinker as Shen Ruolang. Hearing that both these people were music lovers, she thought she'd found a chance to restore her name. So she enthusiastically began explaining that she herself was a singer, and tonight was her chance to make a big impression. A friend had introduced her to a Hong Kong producer. The producer was on his way to Dalian and had to change planes in Beijing. His plane arrived in Beijing just after seven that evening, and he had to spend three hours in the Capital Guesthouse; that's why she was in such a hurry to take a taxi there. If they got on okay, she might have a chance to become a contract singer and become famous.

Shen Ruolang wasn't really interested, but after hearing this story she began to wonder if it really was true. After all, she was supposed to deliver her brother's demo tape to a producer from Hong Kong called Deng. Shen Ruolang didn't know this producer but she'd heard he would make a stopover at the Capital tonight, then fly on to Dalian in the morning. She wasn't sure if this was the same producer that Chen Xiaohong was talking about. Based on Chen Xiaohong's account, this Hong Kong guy would have to get on the plane to Dalian after ten o'clock that same evening, but there weren't any planes from Beijing to Dalian at that late hour. Was there some kind of inconsistency here? The Capital Guesthouse had a special service for receiving guests on stopovers from the airport, so Shen Ruolang knew the flight schedule like the back of her hand.

Whereas Shen Ruolang still had some doubts about Chen Xiaohong because of the inconsistent flight times, Xiao Jianguo was convinced her ridiculous pop-star story was a pack of lies from start to finish. He didn't like her in the first place, and having heard her tortuous explanation, he now distrusted her even more. Wasn't this like an accused thief pointing to the ground and claiming: "I didn't steal three hundred pieces of silver and bury them right in this spot!" Not only did he distrust her, he now thought he had found her weak spot, so from that point on he renewed his verbal assault, making all sorts of indecent insinuations to offend Chen Xiaohong as much as possible, without the slightest scruple. For her part, Chen Xiaohong didn't give an inch, and the two of them sparred back and forth with their sharp tongues, until they completely forgot about the irritation of the traffic jams, and before they knew it the taxi had already reached Sanyuan Bridge.

As soon as they got onto the airport freeway, the taxi left the traffic jams far behind, shooting ahead like greased lighting.

Chen Xiaohong now felt a strong breeze on her face, and worrying that it would mess up her new hairdo, she started rolling up the window. Xiao Jianguo said: "Miss, don't close it. I'm really sorry, but the AC is broken." Chen Xiaohong said: "What sort of wreck are you driving here? We're paying for a Xiali, but this is more like a clapped out old bread van."[1] This time Xiao Jianguo didn't dare to argue, since it was plain that he was at fault. Chen Xiaohong ignored his request and rolled the window all the way up. The taxi suddenly felt stiflingly hot.

Another reason why Chen Xiaohong closed the window was that she wanted to do her makeup. She had finally realized

---

1. "Bread van": small cramped minivans, shaped a bit like a loaf of bread, able to carry up to seven passengers, commonly used as cheap taxis in Beijing in the early- to-mid-1990s, usually painted bright yellow.

that this driver was determined not to believe anything she said. And in any case, a taxi driver was not the kind of person Chen Xiaohong had to try and please, especially since this was probably the last time they would see each other. Nonetheless, for some strange reason, she still resented his attitude. What she hated most was to be scorned by others, especially by people who themselves were no better, but still scorned her just for the sake of feeling superior.

Since she left school, she had met all sorts of people with all sorts of attitudes, and she had soon learned the defensive strategy of treating insults as just so much water off a duck's back. But today was different: today was her big opportunity, and if fate was on her side, this would be her ticket to a bright new future. So she was too agitated to be her usual patient and tolerant self. Yet there wasn't much she could do to fight back. It seemed her only option was to play up how well she was living. The more she was in the presence of people who looked down on her, the more she would make herself up to look dazzling. This was one of her tried and tested formulas. And it just happened that in her hurry to leave home earlier, she hadn't time to put on her makeup. She leaned back in her seat, and giving a wicked smile, fished out her makeup kit.

Today she adjusted her normal makeup routine for strategic reasons. First she doused herself with perfume, hoping to overpower the enemy's initial defenses with an advance burst of fragrance. The perfume wafted around the taxi and didn't disperse. It was a unique scent—even Shen Ruolang couldn't tell what it was. Wrinkling up her nose, she sniffed for quite a while, but apart from the fact that it seemed to get more and more pungent, she wasn't any closer to identifying it. And of course, Xiao Jianguo was irritated by it. Chen Xiaohong inwardly gave a self-satisfied laugh: the reason she knew Xiao Jianguo must be irritated was because he suddenly decided to light a cigarette while still driving at high speed—even though he hadn't smoked earlier during the traffic jam. Also, he turned up the volume on the car stereo. Feeling delighted with herself, Chen Xiaohong thought: *This guy's not so tough after all!* And then the taxi suddenly accelerated and swung into the fast lane. Chen Xiaohong delightedly exclaimed: "Way to go, driver! That's awesome." Xiao Jianguo pretended not to notice, but the taxi soon left the other cars in its wake.

Having completed her perfume-spraying offensive, Chen Xiaohong then fished out her lipstick and holding the mirror in one hand and the lipstick in the other, she began working on the final stages of her facial transformation to the beat of the music. But she found that when it came to doing such intricate work, the taxi, which had seemed so smooth before, was actually swaying quite a bit. Several times, she found herself poising the lipstick before her lips without actually daring to apply it. When the taxi finally slowed down, she was so busy looking in the mirror, she didn't notice it was just a quick toll-booth stop. Just as she began applying the lipstick, the taxi suddenly darted forward, and to make matters worse, it also made a sharp turn to the right and then to the left, followed by a sudden brake to a halt. Chen Xiaohong was flung from side to side by the car's abrupt motions, but fortunately she was wearing her seat belt and was not injured.

"What the hell are you doing!" Chen Xiaohong cried.

"We're here!" Xiao Jianguo announced, poker-faced.

Chen Xiaohong looked around and found they had indeed arrived at the Guesthouse. Collecting herself, she looked back in the mirror and was incensed by what she saw. Just now, when the car had braked, her body was thrust forward, and she had inadvertently painted a thick smear of lipstick across her cheek, forming the right half of a red curly Central Asian-style moustache.

"You stupid jerk!" Chen Xiaohong spat out. Normally when she called people stupid jerks, she didn't really mean it, but this time she was serious. She truly thought this taxi driver was a complete and utter jerk. Still, having said the words, somehow she wasn't satisfied with such a weak curse, and unable to think up a more colorful way to express her true feeling—which was "I really hate your guts, you total and utter jerk-headed dickface!"—she was left with her anger still boiling away inside her. The hotel was right there, and she could easily have gone to the restroom to redo her makeup, but to get out with such a ridiculous painted moustache on would make her a complete laughing stock.

Xiao Jianguo repeated impassively: "We're here."

Chen Xiaohong had no choice but to get out a tissue and wipe her face. But this lipstick was a famous French brand well known for its adhesive qualities, and the only result of her wiping was to spread the moustache into a broad red patch on her right cheek.

Xiao Jianguo now urged her to get a move on: "We've arrived. Aren't you getting out?"

There was a large airport shuttle bus parked right in front of the hotel's revolving door, which Xiao Jianguo couldn't squeeze past, so he had to stop some way from the main entrance. But Shen Ruolang normally went in through the staff entrance, not through the main lobby, and Xiao Jianguo had stopped right beside it. Overwhelmed by the pungent perfume, she was already longing for a chance to escape, and seeing the two of them in front still arguing away, Shen Ruolang looked at the meter which said seventy-eight yuan, fished out forty from her purse and dropped it over the partition to Xiao Jianguo, then opened the door and got out.

Shen Ruolang reached her office right on time, went through the normal procedures for changing shifts, and then logged onto her computer to check the night's guest list so she knew who to expect. Tonight they had two tour groups coming through, one from Hong Kong, the other from Germany, and she made a mental note to have all the alcohol removed from the fridges and mini-bars in the tour groups' rooms. This was because tour groups always left quite early in the morning, and there would be twenty or thirty of them paying their bills at the same time. It would be impossible to check all their minibars. There was also an Air China flight crew coming to overnight at the hotel. Since most of them would be young stewardesses, it was best to give them rooms near the elevators. They'd be sure to come in chattering noisily. Also, they usually had to get up to go back to work when everyone else was still asleep. Apart from these groups, there were also several individual bookings, which Shen Ruolang checked one by one, taking care to make special arrangements for their regular guests.

Shen Ruolang also noted that a Hong Kong guest surnamed Deng had already checked in half an hour ago. Shen Ruolang had not talked to this guest, as he had asked a Beijing agent to reserve his room in advance. The agent frequently made reservations for people at the Guesthouse and knew Shen Ruolang quite well. He had told her: "If you have any professional business to arrange, you should go and talk to this Mr. Deng." Shen Ruolang was wondering what kind of "professional business" she could have, when she suddenly remembered her longhaired brother struggling with his spiritual demons in the semi-underground world of rock music.

Shen Ruolang located Mr. Deng's room number and called him on the telephone. Her plan was first to greet him on behalf of the hotel, to encourage him to contact her if there was anything at all that he needed, and then to ask him when it might be convenient for her to bring over her brother's demo tape. The phone rang several times, but nobody answered—Shen Ruolang guessed he had probably gone to the hotel restaurant for dinner.

Just as she hung up, the hotel's Security Chief pushed open the door and walked in. The personnel arrangements in this hotel were quite interesting in that the head of every department was given the designation of manager, except for the guesthouse security person, who was called the "Chief." Shen Ruolang had long ago pointed out to the current Chief the reason for this: she claimed it was because the aims of Security were not quite the same as those of the hotel, so he couldn't be called a manager. The job of managers was first and foremost to help the hotel make money. Certainly, when Security caught thieves and pickpockets in the hotel it could help improve the hotel's reputation and attract more customers; but when Security went and arrested the "girlfriends" of foreign guests, though the hotel's reputation might remain intact, its chances of attracting many foreign guests were severely diminished. Of course, it wouldn't be so bad if the hotel lost just a few foreign guests of that category, but if most of the foreign guests belonged to "that category," it might have a serious impact on the overall operation of the hotel. When it came right down to it, running a hotel was fundamentally about making money.

But the Security Chief disagreed with her reasoning. He argued that the title "Department Chief" was equivalent to a government official's position, with all its connotations of political power and authority, unlike a "manager," who was simply an employee hired by the hotel. But he said this just for the sake of argument, since he himself knew that he was actually just another employee of the hotel, and he could only act in concert with the law enforcement authorities, lacking the authority to engage in searches and arrests himself.

The reason the Chief had come today was to communicate to her the gist of the government's latest anti-pornography and illicit sexual activities campaign, and to discuss how the various hotel departments should cooperate in implementing it. As soon as Shen Ruolang heard him bringing up this subject yet again, she laughed and said: "The Guest Services Department is only interested in eliminating dirty bacteria from the rooms, not in eliminating dirty magazines and obscenity!" The Security Chief said: "Getting rid of obscenity is a task for the whole society, it's not my private crusade. I don't like getting involved in this either. I'm much better at catching thieves, to tell the truth." Shen Ruolang said: "I didn't mean it like that, I was only wondering how you expect us to 'cooperate'? Just tell me clearly what I should do. Should I tell the staff to reconnoiter the rooms while they are delivering coffee to the guests?"

For a hotel like this, which had many foreign guests, it was really difficult to enforce such government regulations. You couldn't just burst into the rooms and do a search as if it were some two-bit truck stop. Foreigners had this concept called human rights, and even though they accepted that the situation in China was a bit different, they wouldn't put up with random searches that weren't backed up by a shred of evidence to justify them. In those cases, unless you caught them red-handed, they would certainly stand up for their rights. So if you were going to look for obscene behavior in such a hotel, the key was to get accurate leads before acting. This was why the Security Chief was constantly asking for "cooperation" from the Guest Services Department, and reminding the night managers about it. But Shen Ruolang wasn't some kind of private detective, so their endless discussions had never resulted in any concrete action on her part.

When she found out why the chief had come, Shen Ruolang thought to herself: *If they do a search tonight, most likely they'll have a pretty high chance of success. It could be that the girl Chen Xiaohong really is looking for Mr. Deng, and if they find them together, it would be pretty awkward. At the very least, it would upset Mr. Deng and destroy any hope that he'd help out her brother.*

Thinking of Chen Xiaohong and Mr. Deng reminded her of her brother and his CD, but then Shen Ruolang remembered with horror that in her haste to get to the office on time, she had left the disk behind in the taxi's stereo. An agitated expression flashed across her face. If she lost that tape, it would be a disaster: her brother had put all his blood, sweat and tears into getting that CD produced!

At that moment, Chen Xiaohong was sitting at a small table in the hotel's Karaoke bar, far away from the stage, being introduced to a middle-aged man by "Jenny."

Jenny had been a fellow student of Chen Xiaohong's when they first went to middle school and took singing lessons at the Children's Club. It was many years since they graduated from school, and although they had kept in touch, they only contacted each other sporadically when they had to ask a favor or get something done. Whereas Chen Xiaohong was totally focused on being a singer and becoming famous, Jenny had been content with finding hosting jobs in hotels and Karaoke bars, and though she didn't have much driving ambition, she could sometimes still amaze people with her networking ability. She knew that Chen Xiaohong had always wanted to be a professional singer, so she had helped arrange this audition for her. Chen Xiaohong trusted Jenny, so when Jenny told her that this was a rare opportunity, she really believed it was her chance to make it big time.

As soon as Chen Xiaohong entered the hotel, she had gone to find Jenny, but Jenny criticized her for coming so early. She said that Mr. Deng had only just arrived, and they should at least let him get something to eat before starting to discuss business. But as it happened, when they called up to his room, Mr. Deng said that he had just eaten on the plane, so it would be fine for them to meet right away.

Actually, Mr. Deng wasn't expecting to be amazed by Chen Xiaohong's talent. He just didn't feel like being alone, and was looking for someone to have a good time with. Of course, it would be great if she turned out to be a good singer too. And hearing that this girl had such a positive attitude, his curiosity was piqued. He hadn't intended to put on his producer cap while in Beijing, and he hadn't brought his usual retinue of hangers-on to impress people, but after talking to this girl on the phone, he happily and briskly came down to meet her.

Jenny introduced them, then added: "I'll leave you two to chat. If you need anything to drink, just let me know." Jenny turned and went out, leaving Chen Xiaohong gazing at Mr. Deng, wondering how to start the conversation.

Earlier, on the way to the hotel, she had thought of lots of topics to talk about, but somehow they had all slipped her mind. And even if she remembered them, she probably wouldn't have the nerve to open her mouth. What would she say? Ask him about the weather in Hong Kong? How many times had he been to Beijing? Had he visited the Forbidden City, the Temple of Heaven, the Summer Palace? She had plenty of experience in making small talk and getting to know strangers, but that wasn't helping her now. Jenny had assured her that this producer was extremely influential, and he liked to use his influence, so Chen Xiaohong was full of hope for this meeting and had come rushing all the way here just to see him. But having actually met him, she suddenly felt all those petty little topics she'd prepared to break the ice were just so much empty drivel, especially when compared with her true reason for coming.

All these years, she had never quite found the success she longed for, but even in her most difficult times she had always consoled herself by saying: you've got to have patience. But this patience wasn't just a matter of needing time to develop her singing talent; it was also learning how to deal with the people side of the business. There were good singers all over the place, but you could count on the fingers of one hand those who had used their singing talent to become stars. The difference was not in their talent, but in their determination and will to succeed. Chen Xiaohong's voice was not that outstanding, and she had learned to conceal her vocal shortcomings under a sheen of enthusiasm and attitude. But today for some reason she could hardly contain her impatience to find out what this producer thought. Sitting in front of him now, she wanted to blurt out the only question that was on her mind: "So what do you think, am I good enough or not?"

But it was Mr. Deng who calmly smiled at her and spoke first, asking: "So Miss Chen, I've heard you like to sing?" Chen Xiaohong immediately nodded: "Yes, that's right." Hearing Mr. Deng's words, she was able to relax a little. She thought to herself that Jenny's description was pretty accurate: this Mr. Deng doesn't beat around the bush. She then asked: "Would you like to hear me perform a song?" Mr. Deng answered: "Yes, of course, that would be great." Actually Mr. Deng's opening question was meant just to get the conversation rolling, and he was rather startled that she took it as an invitation to sing. Still, it wasn't so surprising that her deep wish to impress him with her voice had caused her to misunderstand him in this way. And what did it matter? He had plenty of time and it might be nice to listen to her singing for a while.

So Chen Xiaohong selected one of the songs on the Karaoke list, and since there weren't many guests in the Karaoke bar, her song came up very quickly. It was a song entitled "The Applause Rang Out," and the first lines went: "I stand all alone on this stage/I hear the applause ring out loud/And my heart overflows with emotion/I've struggled for so many years/To find my way out of the crowd . . ."

Chen Xiaohong had always liked this song, though she couldn't explain clearly why she liked it. She just felt that it encouraged her and motivated her to keep on persevering. Now, as she sang it, she imagined herself standing on a broad stage with the audience staring up at her, rapt and silent, listening to her pouring out her deepest emotions.

After she finished singing there was some applause, but when Chen Xiaohong came out of her reverie and looked around, she found the only person clapping was Mr. Deng.

Chen Xiaohong came down from the platform and sat opposite Mr. Deng, asking: "So what did you think?" "You sing pretty well, Miss Chen, but I don't think that song really suits you. "Why do you say that?" Mr. Deng went on: "You know, that song should be performed by someone who has been through a lot of ups and downs. But you're still so young, and you're just starting out. You should sing songs that are happy and full of energy."

Chen Xiaohong thought to herself: *He has a point, that's something I did kind of feel before, but wasn't able to put my finger on. Even though this song talks about loneliness and struggle, and I have experienced both of those, still my own loneliness and struggling weren't quite in the same league. The person who sings those words should be on the declining end of a great and dazzling career. I still have a long way to go before reaching that point.*

Once more she started to feel downcast, and she couldn't help thinking again of her confrontation just now with that taxi driver.

Just before, when Chen Xiaohong had angrily got out of the cab, and with one hand over her face gone rushing into the hotel, Xiao Jianguo had also got out on his side intending to stop her. He hadn't expected that even with her high heels Chen Xiaohong was still able to run like the wind. Xiao Jianguo tried to catch up, but then he realized that there was a taxi behind him, and the driver was getting fed up. While the two of them had been arguing away inside the taxi, the bus that was blocking the entrance had left. The taxi driver behind them assumed that since they were still sitting in the car, they must be sorting out the fare, and so he just waited patiently. But when he now saw the two of them getting out, one chasing the other, and leaving the taxi right in his way, he got a bit agitated and started blowing his horn repeatedly. And when the next taxi driver in the line, who had no idea what was going on in front, heard the horn blowing, he also started sounding his horn just to add to the noise. Since Xiao Jianguo didn't wish to upset his fellow drivers, he had no choice but to return to his taxi, drive it forward several dozen meters, and stop in front of the main entrance.

When he got out again, the doorman saw him walking up with a furious expression and clenched fists and stopped him. "Who are you looking for?" Xiao Jianguo pointed and said: "Her!" When the doorman looked into the main lobby in the direction Xiao Jianguo was pointing, all he saw was a large tour group that had just arrived and was noisily registering at the desk. He asked again: "Who exactly do you mean?" In Xiao Jianguo's eyes, the only person visible was Chen Xiaohong, and with his angry gaze fixed on her, he continued to try and push his way into the lobby, but the doorman still blocked him. All he could do was stare as Chen Xiaohong's red hair disappeared into a cluster of stores selling warm-colored Central Asian rugs and wall hangings.

"You . . . !" Xiao Jianguo exclaimed, furiously stamping his feet, "Why are you protecting such bad people!"

"Look, just tell me what's going on?" the doorman asked, mystified.

"She took my taxi and didn't pay the fare!" Xiao Jianguo angrily shouted.

Shen Ruolang was sitting with a pained expression on her face. That demo wasn't any CD, it was the original version, and there weren't any copies. Her brother had put a great deal of effort into recording the demo, and now it was lost, just like that. There were thousands of Xiali taxis in Beijing, and Shen Ruolang had no idea where to even begin looking for the one she'd taken. She carefully retraced her journey to work, hoping to pick up clues to help in her search, but nothing sprang to mind. If she'd asked for a receipt, that would have given her something solid to work with, but of course she'd told him she didn't need one. She really regretted sharing a taxi with that girl just for the sake of saving a few lousy dollars, because now she was left with no hope of locating her priceless disk.

Just as she was sitting there feeling sorry for herself, she suddenly became aware of movement in front of her. One of the doormen had come in leading Xiao Jianguo. Shen Ruolang was delighted at this turn of events, and immediately went over to welcome him. For his part, Xiao Jianguo was surprised to find that his other passenger was actually an employee of the hotel, and he greeted her with a smile. Only the doorman was left feeling put out. Seemed like this guy had pulled a fast one on him: he was really looking for Shen Ruolang.

Just now, when Xiao Jianguo had come crazily bursting into the hotel, he claimed some girl had refused to pay her taxi fare. The doorman couldn't let him go in and grab someone just like that, because if they then started arguing or fighting in the lobby, it would be completely unacceptable. In his furious state, Xiao Jianguo couldn't seem to explain things clearly and he ended up shouting: "She's just a common whore and you still let her in your hotel!" When the doorman heard this, he thought it sounded pretty serious, and motivated both by his sense of duty and by a kind of morbid curiosity bred from boredom, he enthusiastically led Xiao Jianguo to the office of the Security Chief. The staff there said that the Chief was over at Guest Services doing some investigative work, so the doorman led Xiao Jianguo over there.

Shen Ruolang shook Xiao Jianguo's hand and said: "Thank you! Thank you for coming! How did you manage to find me?"

Xiao Jianguo looked a bit stunned: "Find you? Why would I want to find you?"

Shen Ruolang said: "Didn't you come to give me back the CD?"

"CD?" After thinking for a while, Xiao Jianguo finally remembered that Shen Ruolang's CD was still in his taxi. "Yes. That's right. I should return the CD. But I don't have it on me right now. Just let me go back and get it."

Standing beside him, the doorman said: "This gentleman is looking for the Chief to report an incident."

Shen Ruolang only then realized that Xiao Jianguo hadn't come to find her, but it didn't really matter. At least she knew the CD wasn't hopelessly lost. So for now she was happy to let him sort out his business, and she didn't interrupt him.

Xiao Jianguo sat in front of them, and the Security Chief said: "We're happy to hear that you can help us with our work. Perhaps you could explain the situation."

Xiao Jianguo then lit a cigarette and started to give a vivid description of how that girl had flagged the taxi down, which route they had taken, what they had talked about on the way, how he had seen from the start that Chen Xiaohong wasn't a good sort, how she had claimed to be coming to the hotel to find the manager of a record company, and who'd believe a complete bald-faced lie like that, and finally, how she had refused to pay her fare when she got out, and had escaped into the hotel. When he had finished, Xiao Jianguo pointed toward Shen Ruolang and said: "If you don't believe me, you can ask this young lady, because she was in the taxi too. She can be my witness."

The Security Chief asked Shen Ruolang: "Can you confirm this?"

"What he said about the taxi ride is basically accurate. Of course, I have no right to speculate on whether those facts actually prove the girl's status. Not paying her fare would certainly demonstrate a lack of honesty on her part, but by that time I had already got out of the taxi, so I'm in no position to confirm that part of the story."

Xiao Jianguo shot an angry glance at her: "Of course the money is a secondary consideration. The key point is that we shouldn't encourage such immoral behavior, don't you agree?"

The Security Chief nodded several times, but he wasn't really convinced. When he first heard that someone had an incident to report, he was very excited, hoping it might be a useful lead in some major organized crime case or something. But when he listened further, he began to feel they were just chasing the wind and clutching at shadows. True, Xiao Jianguo's analysis had its merits, and it could well be that his assumption was correct, but when it came down to it, analysis wasn't the same as hard facts, and even hard facts were subject to different interpretations. Every day, many people like Chen Xiaohong passed through the hotel, and just because you didn't like their appearance, you couldn't then conclude they were one of these or one of those. Still, it was quite likely that the girl hadn't paid her fare, otherwise this guy wouldn't be in such a state.

Having analyzed the situation this far, the Chief decided to place calls to the various departments—the main restaurant, the west wing restaurant, the hotel bar, the swimming pool, the Karaoke bar—asking each whether a girl with red hair was there. He thought it would be best to find the girl at least, and let them confront each other face to face, and have the debtor clear her debts. Of course, if she categorically denied that she hadn't paid, there wasn't much he could do: it was her word against Xiao Jianguo's. But at least doing this would give the girl a bit of a warning: don't think of trying anything else in our hotel, because we have eyes everywhere.

But the feedback from every department was that they hadn't seen such a person. Actually, Chen Xiaohong was still in the Karaoke bar, but luckily for her, Jenny had taken the Chief's call. Jenny guessed they were looking for Chen Xiaohong, but she didn't know what it was about. She thought Chen Xiaohong must have done something pretty bad for them to be chasing her all the way here, and this made it even less likely for her to give the game away. The last thing she wanted was for Chen Xiaohong to be arrested here and possibly get herself into trouble too, so she simply said she hadn't seen her recently. Saying she "hadn't seen her" wasn't quite as dishonest as saying she "wasn't here," and it meant that if Chen Xiaohong happened to get arrested after she went out of the hotel's main entrance, there would no longer be any incriminating connection with herself.

Therefore, having completed a whole round of telephone calls and making no progress at all, the Security Chief had no choice but to apologize to Xiao Jianguo and tell him the girl couldn't be found.

Sitting beside him, Shen Ruolang added, "Perhaps she left already?"

Xiao Jianguo said: "That's not possible. She made such an effort to come all the way here: it would be ridiculous to think she'd leave after less than twenty minutes. What I think is she's already gone into one of your rooms."

The Security Chief said: "If she's really in one of the guestrooms, that makes things more difficult. We can't go searching through the rooms one by one, and finally find her on the fourteenth floor reminiscing about old times with her great auntie."

Xiao Jianguo said: "Of course, she may not be in that line of business. But what if she's some kind of special agent? What if she's already handed over the film from her miniature camera to a foreigner?"

The Security Chief said: "If that was the situation, then it'd be really serious: I would have to notify the National Security Agency immediately. Perhaps, sir, you should knock off work early today and take a break, and I'll let you know when we apprehend her."

Hearing this, Xiao Jianguo realized that he had gone too far and the situation was now out of his hands, and this made him feel disheartened. He looked at the Security Chief, and the Chief looked back at him, and suddenly he sensed that this scene was remarkably similar to the one earlier that afternoon when he had talked to his boss. At that time, the boss's expression was just the same: *we've said everything that needs to be said, so now what?* On the surface Xiao Jianguo was free to make a decision, but what choice did he really have? Feeling frustrated, he sat there with a blank expression, and then said with a touch of self-mockery: "Well since it's like that, there's not much else I can do. In any case, I guess I've fulfilled my duty to society."

The Security Chief said: "Yes, that's right. Improving the moral fiber of society is something that requires the cooperation of every upstanding citizen." He then gave a pointed glance in Shen Ruolang's direction, as if to say: see this guy, he's got a clearer grasp of the problem than you have! Shen Ruolang pretended she hadn't noticed.

Then as Xiao Jianguo got up to leave, Shen Ruolang said, "I'll come with you to pick up the CD, okay?" The two of them then each played a polite little game, one insisting that it would be too much trouble for her to come out and he'd go get it for her; the other insisting that it would be too much trouble for him to come back in again and it was no trouble for her to get it herself, etc., etc. In the end, Xiao Jianguo's politeness was no match for Shen Ruolang's because she was desperate not to let the CD disappear again.

After she heard the Security Chief making all those telephone calls, Shen Ruolang felt a bit put out. She was inclined to agree with Xiao Jianguo's interpretation, in other words, that Chen Xiaohong had already entered one of the guest rooms, but she didn't know if it was Mr. Deng's room or not. If it really was his room, then she began to have doubts about whether she should put her brother in Mr. Deng's hands. Despite having worked for so many years, and despite knowing that someone's sexual peccadillos did not necessarily affect that person's ability to do his job, as soon as Shen Ruolang realized that Mr. Deng was probably a womanizer, she couldn't help feeling that it made things awkward. And awkwardness is such an irrational feeling that no amount of persuasive reasoning can overcome it.

So as she walked behind Xiao Jianguo, Shen Ruolang remained silent and gloomy. Xiao Jianguo was also brooding, although his mood was a bit different. He was depressed that Chen Xiaohong hadn't been caught, and those two hotel officials going on about "money" this and "money" that had really stuck in his craw. True, Chen Xiaohong hadn't paid him the fare, but it wasn't just about the money. If she had been a robber or a thug and had refused to pay, he would have just treated it as a stroke of fate and let it pass. That would have been an obvious case of evil versus good, black versus white. If his whiteness could not defeat that kind of blackness, what could he say? But Chen Xiaohong wasn't like that, she was a person like him, yet she still wanted to cheat him. It wasn't really that she was a single individual who wanted to cheat him, it was more like she represented a kind of force against him. In other words, viewed as an individual, she may have had a few black spots on her character, but overall she was still more or less white. Yet when you linked her together with everyone else, they formed this immense gray force arrayed against him. And who were all these other people? His boss? The Security Chief? That woman walking behind him? In some ways they were part of it, but in some ways not—Xiao Jianguo couldn't put his finger on it. He just felt that he was stuck in a gray world, a world that one couldn't describe clearly but which went to enormous lengths to make life difficult for him. Xiao Jianguo did his best to fight back against that world, but right now he couldn't even work out where he should aim his blows.

In silence they walked to the parking lot, and Xiao Jianguo wound down the window from the outside, put his arm in and searched for the disk. As he fished around without finding it, he felt a cool breeze wafting out from inside the taxi. He was astonished, and switching on the light to look more carefully, he found that he had accidentally pressed the wrong button and turned on the air-conditioning. This air-conditioning system really seemed to break down for no reason at all, and then just as mysteriously fix itself. He got in the taxi and looked here and there, but he was unable to find an explanation. Of course, he ignored the fact that Shen

Ruolang was left standing outside.

Shen Ruolang bent down and asked: "What's the problem?" At this, Xiao Jianguo finally remembered she was there, took the CD out, and passed it to her. Shen Ruolang took it, thanked him, and seeing that Xiao Jianguo didn't respond, turned and walked away. After going a couple of paces, she couldn't help looking back again to see what Xiao Jianguo was doing, but he was still sitting there like a dummy, with the taxi door wide open and cold air wafting out in regular bursts. The light was still on, and she could clearly see the dashboard with all its controls, but Xiao Jianguo himself was just a vague silhouette. All this seemed pretty weird in the middle of the huge pitch-black parking lot. Hesitantly, Shen Ruolang called out: "Thanks again for giving us that lead. But I can't guarantee we'll be able to make good on her fare."

The silhouette turned its head and said slowly: "You know, money isn't necessarily the main thing. As long as she's caught I won't feel quite so resentful." He said this in a slightly gruesome way that gave Shen Ruolang the creeps. Shen Ruolang was not someone with deep psychological insight, and all she could think was: how can losing a paltry forty yuan make him so vengeful? She couldn't make sense of it no matter how hard she tried, but somehow the situation upset her, so she turned around and walked quickly toward the hotel, intent on getting back to her office as fast as she could.

Another reason she walked quickly was because of the weather. It was the hottest and most humid time of the year, and even though it was already eight or nine in the evening, there wasn't the slightest trace of cool or dry air. On top of that, she had been working in her air-conditioned office, and coming out suddenly like this was just like getting steamed in a pot. But the more she hurried, the longer the path seemed to stretch out. Walking and walking, she suddenly heard a great roaring noise as a plane flew right overhead toward the north. Because the hotel was so close to the airport, the planes were still really low when they passed over, and as she looked up, Shen Ruolang felt as if she could almost see the people inside the cabin windows.

This plane was about to land. By this hour, it was unlikely that any planes would be taking off, especially planes heading toward Dalian. Shen Ruolang reminded herself again and again: "You must be careful, really careful. You absolutely must not ruin your brother's prospects."

When Shen Ruolang returned to her office, the Security Chief asked her what was so important about that CD. She was about to tell the truth, but then thought it might be inappropriate, so she just changed the subject. While walking back, she had already decided on a plan of action, which was first of all to find out exactly what kind of person this Mr. Deng really was. So now she told the Security Chief that she had found a clue from the registration records that the producer Chen Xiaohong was looking for could be a man surnamed Deng from Hong Kong. The Security Chief placed a call to the floor staff asking them whether this Mr. Deng was in his room, but they said he had gone downstairs, probably to eat dinner. The Security Chief and Shen Ruolang exchanged glances, and then the Chief ordered the person on the line: "Keep an eye on his room for any signs of movement. If he comes back by himself let me know, and if he comes back with someone else let me know as well; also tell me if he comes back first and then someone else follows later."

Chen Xiaohong had absolutely no idea that so many people were tailing her. Oblivious to everything around her, she just continued to sing one song after another, in every style and on every topic. At first there weren't many people in the bar, but her singing attracted several male guests who were happy to sit and listen to her. When it got to ten o'clock, the Karaoke bar really started to fill up with a great mixture of people of every shape and color, and Chen Xiaohong was no longer able to monopolize the stage.

Only at this point did she realize just how long she had been singing, and that it was probably time for Mr. Deng to leave. Feeling a bit alarmed, she asked him: "Shouldn't you be thinking about heading for the airport?" But Mr. Deng's answer surprised her: "My plane doesn't leave till ten in the morning, so it's okay if I stay up a bit late tonight." Hearing this, Chen Xiaohong thought, *That can't be right. When did he change his flight?*

Mr. Deng had not changed his flight at all. It was Jenny who had falsely reported his schedule. Jenny was very familiar with the mindset of aspiring singers, and their tendency to be willing to do anything to get ahead, especially in the case of singers like Chen Xiaohong who were not blessed with outstanding natural talent. But she also didn't want Chen Xiaohong to lose face in front of her. By pretending that she wasn't aware of Mr. Deng's flight schedule, she gave Chen Xiaohong a chance to say goodbye to her and leave the bar with Mr. Deng, and then they could head upstairs together—if that's what they planned to do. Chen Xiaohong was quite bright, and having heard Mr. Deng's response, she immediately realized the implications of the situation. Certainly one couldn't fault Jenny for her careful planning, but there was just one thing she hadn't bargained for—that people may decide to change.

Even though Chen Xiaohong had spent many years fighting to get ahead in the real world, she still thought of herself as a person with a vision. Her vision wasn't fixed too high: what she wanted most of all was to perform on the stage, and to have her name and her songs appear on promotional posters. She had first formed her vision when still in high school. Back then she had secretly fallen in love with a boy in her class, but the boy remained completely oblivious to her feelings. Feeling the pain of unrequited love, Chen Xiaohong had constantly imagined herself standing on a lofty revolving stage. The stage was surrounded by seats in curved rows, with multicolored spotlights shining down from above, and Chen Xiaohong stood there singing her songs full of pain and intense emotion. In the darkness among the crowds below, possibly he was there, possibly not. It didn't really matter. She could always find some way to convey the message to him, perhaps through some kind of newspaper announcement, that she was singing these songs for him and him alone. Yes, they were all for him, every sentence was formed with their special love in mind, and every phrase would strike directly and piercingly at his heart. But there was a problem: if this was the reason for her singing, then why did she not imagine herself in a single private room, with one candle burning, singing to him alone in the dim flickering light? She had never once pictured a scene like that. Her dreams of love were always inseparably tied to performing onstage. It would be more appropriate for her to express her feelings in an intimate whisper, but she always chose to make a public declaration. Why did she do this? She was a sensitive person, and had realized this problem long ago, but she had no explanation for it.

After graduating from high school, Chen Xiaohong began singing in Karaoke halls and lounges on the provincial performing circuit, but no matter whether she was singing at a Beijing venue or on some hastily constructed stage out in the sticks, she was never able to find the stage she had seen in her vision, or feel the way her imagination told her she should feel. It seemed she would never have the opportunity to perform on a big-time show-business stage. Getting that opportunity became a kind of obsession, and for a while she completely forgot about her search for love. The entertainment world is based on fame and profit, and if despite your struggle you can't become famous, you have no value at all. And when you yourself have no value, your feelings have even less value. So Chen Xiaohong couldn't be bothered to deal with her feelings. She didn't even try to analyze all the contradictions within her heart.

But today, sitting next to Mr. Deng, Chen Xiaohong suddenly had an epiphany.

Earlier, when she had greeted Mr. Deng with a handshake, for a brief moment she had felt a burst of pride in her heart. She saw herself as a future singing star shaking hands with a great producer. This feeling lasted only an instant, and then her mind returned from the future to the present, but this mysterious inner swelling, so difficult to describe, momentary as it was, gave her a taste of glory, yes, that was the word: "glory"!

And enlightened by that word glory, she also was suddenly able to unravel the knot that had bound her heart for so many years. What she wanted was this: to dress up her declarations of love and give them depth and grandeur. Chen Xiaohong had always believed the old saying that "the words of ordinary people have little influence," but when she stood on a glorious stage, suddenly she became much more powerful and her love seemed so much more profound.

One could say this was a sudden realization, but at the same time it wasn't so sudden. Certainly this sensation of glory had formed just now in an instant; but her belief about the meager influence of ordinary words was the result of many years of bitter experience and struggle. Yet what Chen Xiaohong now had finally understood was that all along, behind her search for success, she was really searching for love. And with this realization came a renewed sense of self-respect. She was well aware of what she had done these past few years in her life as an entertainer. The contemptuous attitude of people like Xiao Jianguo toward her was not completely unfounded. But today, with her sudden new sense of self-esteem, she felt betrayed by all of Jenny's careful arrangements. This Jenny—what kind of low-down person does she think I am? How could she do such a thing to me?

Just then Jenny happened to come along bringing the drinks they had ordered. Having been neglected for most of the evening, Mr. Deng was thinking to himself: *what a silly idiot she is, singing all evening without a break.* But though he thought this, he wasn't really annoyed with Chen Xiaohong. He just felt she was a bit timid. So he decided to take advantage of Jenny's appearance with the drinks to say a few words to Chen Xiaohong. Though he already knew the answer, he asked her: "You sing pretty well Miss Chen. Where are you working?"

"I'm a performing artist, so I've sung at all kinds of venues." Chen Xiaohong purposely emphasized the words "performing artist" and "sung."

"Singing takes a lot of work, doesn't it?"

"Of course singing is hard work, but your success

depends on your talent, unlike, say, being a bar hostess."
Chen Xiaohong was feeling angry, and seeing Jenny there
she couldn't resist the urge to insult her. Jenny pretended
she didn't know what was really going on, and making as if
she was offended, patted her on the back and said: "Listen
to Miss Chen here. She can get by with her great voice, so
she looks down on bar hostesses like me. Well whatever, I'm
never going to make it. And since Mr. Deng obviously knows
how to spot talent, I might as well just leave you two alone."

Jenny's pat on the back was actually quite a heavy slap,
so hard that it hurt her own hand. Feeling the sharp pain
of the slap, Chen Xiaohong knew that Jenny was not just
pretending to be annoyed.

Back in the office, it was already twelve o'clock, and the
seconds and minutes gradually passed by as they waited.

Shen Ruolang had other things to work on, and she
completed her tasks as she waited. But the Security Chief was
focusing all his attention on waiting for that telephone call.
Suddenly he began to feel it was a bit pointless and wondered
whether his intuition was wrong. Perhaps it wasn't what they
thought after all, he reflected gloomily. And on the other
hand, even if he was right, it seemed like a big waste of time
to him. He had been looking for a lead like this all along, but
he wasn't sure if it was even worth the effort to follow it up.
What made investigation fun was the suspense. And to burst
through the door regardless of the consequences—search first
and ask questions later: that was what gave him the biggest
kick. He glanced over at Shen Ruolang, conscientiously
writing something in a little notebook, as if she had absolutely
no concern about the outcome of this incident.

Actually, Shen Ruolang was feeling extremely tense.

Subconsciously she had already bound the fate of her brother tightly together with the moral character of Mr. Deng. On the one hand, she feared that their suspicions were true, but on the other hand, she was desperate to ferret out the truth. One aspect of her character that she had always been proud of was that she never tried to hide her head in the sand like an ostrich. It gave her a kind of irrational pleasure to find out the painful truth, like the pleasure one gets from picking off a scab even though one knows it will hurt. But of course, at the same time, she also secretly hoped against hope that just maybe the "scab" would have already healed itself.

There was another person who was worrying about Chen Xiaohong, and that was Xiao Jianguo.

Xiao Jianguo had decided after some consideration to just wait there. He didn't believe that Chen Xiaohong had already left. He wanted to see her with his own eyes walking out of the hotel, and then rush up and grab her. Best of all would be if there was a man with her, then he could interrogate them, asking them each what the name of the other was, since they'd be sure not to know, and making them feel thoroughly humiliated. He forgot that he himself didn't know their names, so he wouldn't be able to confirm their answers. And in fact he didn't bother to think out his plan very carefully at all, since he even wasn't at all certain that he'd be able to catch Chen Xiaohong by herself, let alone with a john. But he just felt this irrepressible impulse, mixed with countless other feelings of injustice and resentment. Today, on this cruelly hot summer night, there was absolutely no way he was going to suppress all these feelings.

He was definitely not doing this for the money, since he didn't know how long he would have to wait—perhaps even the whole night. If that happened, then for the sake of getting back his forty yuan, he would have missed the chance to earn another several hundred. But he also knew that it *was* something to do with the money. After all, it was Chen Xiaohong's refusal to pay the fare that had finally caused all the accumulated fury lying dormant inside him to erupt. So there was some connection between the cause and the effect that he couldn't quite explain. His mind seemed to be constantly shifting its state from clear to muddied, and then back again. His greatest wish now was to catch Chen Xiaohong as soon as possible, and maybe at the moment he laid his hands on her all his feelings of frustration would finally evaporate. So he redoubled his effort to keep his eyes wide open and pinned on the hotel entrance.

At first he kept the window open, because the air in the suburbs was at least a little bit cooler than the air downtown, and also because he had little confidence in the miraculous recovery of the air conditioning system—anyway it was already after midnight. But leaving the window open led to another problem: mosquitoes. And since the mosquitoes in the suburbs were wilder than those downtown, his arms and face were soon covered in large spots. When his legs also started itching, it was clear that the mosquitoes were not just attacking the parts of his body exposed to the outside, but had managed to get right inside the taxi. The itchiness wasn't the worst part: it was the noise they made that was really unbearable, a tedious yet persistent little whining. Xiao Jianguo found that sound totally exasperating.

Finally he decided to wind up the window and switch on the air conditioning. Most of the mosquitoes were then blocked outside the taxi, though a few were still trapped inside. At first these few trapped individuals buzzed around him, tentatively testing their chances, then they started to make a concerted attack. Xiao Jianguo took a blanket from the back seat to cover himself and turned the air conditioning even higher. And strangely, now the air conditioning was working extremely well, so as the taxi's interior grew steadily cooler, gradually those few mosquitoes also ran out of energy and ceased their attacks.

Xiao Jianguo felt a kind of pleasure he had never experienced before. All the disappointments and humiliations of the day seemed to evaporate just as the mosquitoes gradually lost their ability to fly. His mood was now much more peaceful, and catching Chen Xiaohong seemed to be merely a little game, a game that he might as well finish since he had already started it. With his eyes still wide open, he continued to watch the hotel in the distance, but at the same time he also started to notice the stars in the sky between the taxi and the hotel. The stars were so beautiful, and he could enjoy the view of the summer night without being bitten by all those mosquitoes. That was the benefit of air conditioning. But suddenly he remembered: he'd heard someone say one shouldn't leave a car's air conditioning running for too long because it could be dangerous. Who said that again? Seemed he couldn't recall. His brain didn't seem to be functioning properly, as if it had stopped. Oh yes, it was the boss who told him. Well he could go to hell: when did he ever help him? Who believed his damn nonsense. He was just trying to stop me from bugging him about getting the air conditioning fixed. It's true I wouldn't normally use it much even if it was fixed, but that's to save the gas. Still, today is different, today I want to indulge myself a bit, and kill off a few mosquitoes. Today I'm happy.

Xiao Jianguo kept on looking sleepily ahead, but he felt his neck was already getting stiff. He had already lost the ability to respond to his bodily sensations. He sank into a dream world. In his mind, he kept on repeating to himself: Today I'm happy.

By two AM, the guests were gradually dispersing from the Karaoke bar. Mr. Deng, seeing that this Miss Chen wasn't interested in taking things any further, suppressed his wandering desires and returned to his room feeling frustrated. Jenny directed some of the staff to clear up the cups and plates, and after turning off the sound system in the control room she came out and saw Chen Xiaohong sitting in a corner looking very lonely.

There are many people in this world who seem to shrink from success. In other words, before they find success some kind of strange demonic urge makes them suddenly throw it all away. Like when someone spends a whole year working their tails off to prepare for an exam, but just before the exam they suddenly get sick: that's a classic case of shrinking from success. Some might call it fate. Indeed, Jenny believed that one's character was actually one's fate. In Jenny's eyes, this Chen Xiaohong was a prime example of someone shrinking from success: she had seemed so in touch with the real world, but then suddenly had become so ridiculously romantic. She should have seen that this was just the black night before the dawn, but unfortunately she was too tied up in her feelings to realize it. That was the cruel thing about life: those in the thick of it can only see one side, either complete darkness, or complete dawn. Chen Xiaohong had expected only the dawn—not just the dawn but the risen sun at eight or nine in the morning, or the blazing midday sun "gloriously" shining down on her.

Jenny couldn't help feeling sorry for her. She had sincerely tried to help her, but the pity was that their expectations were different. She also realized that Chen Xiaohong resented what she'd done and felt that she had gone too far. She wanted to apologize, but was worried that the more she explained things the worse she would seem. Chen Xiaohong didn't feel like talking to her either, so for a while they just looked at each other without speaking. Eventually it was Jenny who broke the ice saying: "It's so late now, how are you getting home?"

"How am I getting home? Huh, well, at least there's still one person who cares about me." Chen Xiaohong could never keep up her dignified airs very long. And having cast away her illusions of success, she had now immediately re-assumed her normal cheeky attitude. She continued: "I spent most of my money on these clothes, and then you told me that Mr. Deng was only here for three hours, and I was so scared of being late that I splurged on a Xiali taxi to get here. Now I don't even have enough for a taxi back home." Having said this, she suddenly remembered that actually she hadn't paid the fare for her Xiali taxi, and recalling once again the ridiculous image of that taxi driver, she felt that she had at least got *something* out of this evening, and this made her giggle. Seeing her laughing, Jenny relaxed a bit. Of course she didn't believe her damned story about not having enough for a taxi; and she knew Chen Xiaohong really wanted to chat with her for a while, just like when they were at school together and they would often chatter away all night. So she suggested: "Well you don't need to go home tonight, do you? Why not stay in my off-hours dormitory, and then you can take the seven o'clock hotel shuttle downtown in the morning and catch a bus back home from there, okay?" Chen Xiaohong, of course, agreed immediately.

Right around the same time, the floor staff called the Security Chief to tell him that Mr. Deng had returned by himself. Half an hour later, the staff called again to say that no other people, in fact not even a mosquito, had gone into Mr. Deng's room yet. The Security Chief told them to "keep watching," and then he said goodbye to Shen Ruolang and returned to his office.

Only now was Shen Ruolang finally able to relax her tight grip on her feelings. She sat alone in her office for some time, feeling quite agitated. Finally, as daybreak came, she found herself overcome by an irresistible urge to sleep, so she lay down on the table intending to have a rest. She didn't really mean to fall asleep, and according to the regulations she wasn't allowed to sleep. But maybe because she had been too tense all night, it wasn't very long before she entered the world of dreams.

In her dreams, the famous singer Zhang Chu pushed open the door and walked in. Shen Ruolang went forward to greet him, and shaking his hand said: "How are you, Zhang Chu. I loved your song "Big Sister," I really loved it. But how come you haven't composed any great songs since then?" Zhang Chu laughed and said: "Sister, who says I haven't composed great songs? Why do you think I came here if not to bring you my new special collection?" "That's nonsense—I'm not your sister!" Then Zhang Chu took off his shades. "Take another look, and tell me who I am." As soon as she looked again, Shen Ruolang saw that it wasn't Zhang Chu at all, but her brother, no doubt about it. She held his hands and carefully looked him up and down. Her brother was now dressed in fancy trendy clothes and his hair was cut into a clean fresh style. "Well you've really made it this time!" Shen Ruolang exclaimed, delighted.

Shen Ruolang had never actually experienced the sweet taste of success herself. She'd always known that her talents were mediocre, and instead she'd placed all her hopes on her brother's shoulders. Now that they had actually come true in her beautiful dream, she felt delighted yet also sad, and before she knew it she was weeping.

Her tears wet the rims of her eyes and this in turn woke her up. She sat up recalling the dream she just had, and realized she was getting too worked up about delivering the CD. She consoled herself, "Don't worry, Mr. Deng is a reliable person." But within her heart she still felt unsettled, not necessarily because of Mr. Deng but maybe because of some other unresolved matter.

Her agitated feeling drove her out of the office. At daybreak the hotel was extremely quiet. Shen Ruolang walked through the restaurant, the Karaoke bar, the wine bar, and the gym— nothing seemed amiss. She then proceeded aimlessly toward the main entrance, where a different doorman from the one she met the night before was on duty. This doorman opened the door for her, and she went out and stood under the awning.

The sun had already risen in the east, a fiery red ball, promising yet another scorching hot day. But the night had still not completely receded, and there were still little pockets of coolness in the air. As she stood in the midst of a pale gray morning mist, Shen Ruolang suddenly noticed a red Xiali parked in the parking lot. Normally, taxi drivers didn't spend the night there, and it was surely too early to be waiting for early morning guests departing. Suddenly a thought flashed through Shen Ruolang's mind: *It couldn't still be that same driver could it?* Having thought it, she at once felt it was ridiculous, but at the same time her curiosity got the better of her, and she found herself walking over there.

She crouched down at the window and peered inside, and she saw Xiao Jianguo in there, stareing back at her. But his face was a purply blue color, his two eyes were tightly closed, and his mouth was wide open, as if he was shouting something. Shen Ruolang was completely stunned, and for a moment thought she must still be dreaming.

That whole morning, the Security Chief was kept running his feet off. Who would have thought that taxi driver who reported the incident last night would be found dead here? He regretted not having made more effort, since now the driver had died without getting his lost fare back, he would certainly not go to his grave peacefully. His guilty conscience impelled the Chief to work even harder, reporting the situation to Public Security, notifying the taxi company, and keeping the hotel's top executives up-to-date, and while he informed all these other people he continued to search for more information to fill in the gaps in his own knowledge. He begged Shen Ruolang to give him some assistance, but she was completely hardhearted, and had decided to take the early bus back home and go to sleep.

By the time Shen Ruolang had finished her shift, it was already seven thirty. She had gone to the hotel café and found Mr. Deng eating there. After introducing herself and explaining the situation, she gave him her brother's little demo disk. Mr. Deng promised that he would listen to it carefully after he got home, and would tell her what he thought. Shen Ruolang repeatedly expressed how grateful she was for his help. Having finished this piece of business, she went to the hotel's main entrance, where the first shuttle bus to downtown was already waiting. As soon as she got on board, she discovered that Chen Xiaohong was sitting there in the back row. Her heart missed a beat and she thought to herself: *This girl spent the night at the hotel after all!*

Chen Xiaohong and Jenny had talked through the whole night, completely forgetting about going to sleep. They were still chattering when Jenny had suddenly said: "Oh no, the bus is about to leave," at which point Chen Xiaohong finally noticed that it had been light for quite some time. So she scrambled to put on her clothes and rushed out to the hotel entrance. By now she had completely returned to her normal state of mind, and as she sat in the bus waiting for it to leave, she began putting on her makeup and thinking about what she would do today. Because she hadn't had any sleep, her face was looking a bit rough, so she spread the make-up on a bit thicker than usual. She was just getting out her lipstick to complete the final stage of the process when Shen Ruolang got on the bus.

Shen Ruolang's appearance gave Chen Xiaohong a huge start, and her heart began to beat faster. After all, Shen Ruolang was a witness who could testify that she had spent the night at the hotel, and even though she had done nothing wrong, Shen Ruolang wouldn't know that. Therefore, seeing Shen Ruolang's expression, Chen Xiaohong felt embarrassed and guilty. Her agitation made her hands unsteady, and once again she inadvertently painted a lipstick moustache above her mouth.

This time, applied to her over-powdered face, the moustache seemed all the more obtrusive. Finally Shen Ruolang understood that she really did dislike this girl, and despite the fact that she still placed her in the category of "guest," it didn't help her overcome her disgust this time. Lipstick, if applied to the lips, might easily be seen as emphasizing their natural color. But once it has left the region of the mouth, one can no longer escape its stark redness. As that dazzling and irritating color glowed in front of her eyes, Shen Ruolang thought to herself: *That must be where the old saying comes from: beautiful ruddy faces will surely lead to disaster!* Having satisfactorily "labeled" Chen Xiaohong in this way, she then gave her a contemptuous look. And having done that, she felt much more contented. She went and found herself a window seat. As for Chen Xiaohong, she took out some tissue paper and rubbed her face with it repeatedly. She still hadn't finished cleaning her face when the bus started moving.

Chen Xiaohong knew nothing about Xiao Jianguo's death, so seeing that look of contempt, she assumed Shen Ruolang still despised her for being one of "those kinds of women." And if truth be told, Chen Xiaohong had almost proved her right. Recalling the events of the previous night, suddenly they seemed so far away.

It was yet another blazing hot sunny morning. The sun made the buildings on either side of the highway sparkle. When Chen Xiaohong had come along this stretch of road the previous night, the sun was already setting and those blocks of buildings had appeared to her just like rows of mountain peaks. Now, under the clear morning light, she truly felt that the buildings were totally man-made. Looking at them as they rushed past her, she saw steel-reinforced concrete, walls of glass, and blue-glazed tiled roofs. Suddenly the thought came to her that if she simply worked steadily, adding one brick and one tile at a time, wouldn't she find her success in the end? But then she also thought: *No, when it comes down to it, people are not bricks and tiles. They're a lot weaker and more fragile. Bricks and tiles can wait for a hundred years or a thousand years, but people just don't have time to hang around, following the prescribed order; that's why they always use their brains to find shortcuts. People use their brains to think. But at the same time, because they think too much, sometimes this prevents them from just doing things.* Wasn't she herself a prime example of this?

Chen Xiaohong kept looking up at those towering skyscrapers glistening like fish-scales, pushing past her like surging wind-blown clouds. She felt sad, but also proud, and this powerful mix of emotions inexorably overflowed into tears running down her face.

DECEPTION

THAT WHOLE SUMMER, WHENEVER LIN DUODUO WENT out she wore a pair of tea-colored sunglasses. The sun blazed down fiercely from the sky, and the heat pulsated up from the ground. If she didn't have those shades to protect her, Lin Duoduo would have gone completely nuts. But shades had their defects too: they made her eyes feel stifled, as if they needed to breathe.

Luckily, autumn was here and university classes were starting again. Lin Duoduo no longer had to wear her shades.

Still, she put them on again the day she went to the campus post office. The most common method of sending money was through the postal savings bank, and since it was only the second week of the new term, the place was packed with customers. The heat and odor emanating from all these people inevitably reminded Lin Duoduo of summer again. She was holding a wire transfer receipt in her left hand, so she stuck her right hand into her handbag and fished out her shades. There were so many people sorting out their business in the post office that the queue snaked all the way down the hall. Lin Duoduo put on her shades and looked down at her wire transfer receipt, turning it over and studying it carefully.

One thousand yuan—enough to cover ten months of Lin Duoduo's living costs. Seen through her shades, the receipt looked darker, as if it was years old. She had pushed summer out of the way; autumn was the season in which to reap her reward. Surprisingly she felt quite calm now that she had all this money.

Lin Duoduo was studying at the Foreign Languages Academy. She constantly saw notices posted up on campus which, without directly stating it, made it clear they were looking for bright students to take exams on behalf of other people. Whatever exam you could think of—TOEFL tests, GRE, professional exams, English proficiency tests—there always seemed to be people willing to pay someone else to take the exams for them.

Previously, when she had run short of money, Lin Duoduo was often tempted to take up this offer, but her scruples always got the better of her. That summer vacation, all her classmates had gone home, leaving her all alone in her dorm room. And in her loneliness, she had lost her moral compass . . .

Someone tapped her on the shoulder. Awakened from her daydreams, Lin Duoduo turned to see her class representative, Du Juan.

"I saw a wire transfer receipt for you in the department mailroom," Du Juan said.

"Yeah, got it," Lin Duoduo replied, unconsciously grasping the receipt more tightly. "My mom sent me some pocket money."

"But the sender is in Beijing. I thought your home was in Guangxi Province?"

"My mom has a friend in Beijing who owes her money." Fine beads of sweat were forming on Lin Duoduo's forehead. Why were so many people lined up here?

"Since she's here in Beijing, why is she wasting all that

effort wiring the money? Why not just deliver it by hand?"
Du Juan's expression was just like a lawyer grilling a reluctant
witness.

"I was afraid she'd rip me off with counterfeit notes!"
Her response sounded so sincere that Du Juan was finally
convinced and nodded her head. Lin Duoduo now took the
initiative: "Looks like you've finished what you came here to
do. No need to hang around waiting for me."

"I just got things sorted out a minute ago," Du Juan said
with a sincere expression of regret: "If only you'd seen me
up front a bit sooner, you could have joined me and saved all
this waiting!"

"No problem. I'm not in any hurry," Lin Duoduo replied.
She smiled politely, but couldn't help fidgeting with her
sunglasses.

"I'm in no hurry either," Du Juan said with a dazzling
smile. The line was slowly but surely edging its way forward,
and Du Juan patiently moved forward keeping pace beside
it. Ever since the new term began, Du Juan had been looking
for a chance to chat with Lin Duoduo, but whenever she had
tried to start a conversation, Lin Duoduo had made some
excuse and gone off. Today, fortune was on her side.

Du Juan was right in the thick of planning a grand strategy
that would benefit everybody, Lin Duoduo included. They
were all starting their final year, and lots of students were
contacting foreign universities, hoping to do their graduate
studies overseas. If they wanted to go abroad, besides passing
various entrance exams, they also had to include university
transcripts in their applications. The problem was, quite a
few students had slackened off after getting into university:
they thought it was enough just to scrape by in their courses.
Now that they were applying to foreign universities, they

realized too late that their Chinese grades could sink them.

The only solution was to find a way to forge their grades. It has been an open secret in many universities these past few years that grades were being altered. Lots of people were definitely doing it, although no one seemed to know for sure who these people were. Because no one wanted to admit what they were doing, everyone found their own way to do it, and everyone suspected everyone else. In Du Juan's eyes, this was a great waste of resources. Her brilliant plan was to get everyone to work together to rationalize the whole grade altering process. This would save everyone a lot of effort and money, and overcome the poisonous atmosphere of mutual suspicion and competition.

Some classmates were desperate to change their grades, while others didn't seem too concerned if they were changed or not; but since Du Juan claimed she had access to the facilities to make changes for everyone, both these groups were happy to go along with her scheme. Only a tiny minority of students whose grades were already excellent didn't need to alter them, and these students greeted Du Juan's proposal with cold indifference. Lin Duoduo belonged to this tiny minority.

The previous week, which was the second day of the new semester, Du Juan had collared Duoduo in the cafeteria and made the following proposal: "Duoduo, your grades are good. You may think you don't need to change them. But if everyone else is changing theirs, it wouldn't be fair to you, would it? That's why we've all agreed to increase our GPAs by a maximum of 0.3, which means people like you who already have good grades won't fall back in the rankings. Does that sound reasonable?"

"I couldn't care less how much you increase or decrease

them," Lin Duoduo replied, picking out a hunk of meat from her bowl and discarding it on the table.

"Have you become a vegetarian?" Du Juan asked.

"My family is in mourning. When someone dies among our people, we're not allowed to eat meat for the whole three-day mourning period."

Du Juan then recalled that Lin Duoduo was from Guangxi Province. She wanted to ask "Who died in your family?" but not being from the same ethnic group, she wasn't sure how to do it without offending her. The Zhuang minority people lived in Guangxi, didn't they? Was Lin Duoduo one of them? She looked down the long dining table and saw little piles of chicken bones, spinach stems, and other leftovers. They reminded her of grave mounds on a barren plain. Du Juan felt a twinge of remorse that she had steered the conversation in this direction.

So that little conversation had gone nowhere, and the next time she talked to Duoduo wasn't any more productive. Their conversations always seemed to branch off in unexpected directions. Du Juan sensed that Lin Duoduo had changed, and she could no longer grasp what was going on inside her head. What had really happened to Duoduo that summer?

Back to the line. The people in front moved forward a step, but Lin Duoduo, lost in her thoughts, didn't seem to notice. Du Juan gave her a nudge and Lin Duoduo suddenly came to her senses and closed the gap.

Du Juan stayed right behind Lin Duoduo, and as they moved she patted her satchel and whispered to Duoduo: "I just picked up the set of seals today."

Counterfeit seals were essential tools for altering the grade reports. As the main organizer and sponsor of this scheme, Du Juan had previously guaranteed to everyone that she could obtain a set of perfect seals indistinguishable from the real thing. It seemed she had done it.

This piece of news piqued Lin Duoduo's curiosity. "Who did you get to carve them?"

"It's no good getting new ones carved! These ones have been used by previous students for three consecutive years now. They're practically cultural relics. Their authenticity has never once been challenged!" Du Juan looked expectantly at Lin Duoduo: "How about it? Are you in?"

Lin Duoduo shook her head. A mysterious smile played languidly on her lips.

This smile irritated Du Juan: "What's up with you? Seems to me over this one summer break you've turned into an idiot!"

Lin Duoduo's eyes, gazing back to the recent past, remained hidden behind her tea-colored shades.

That day had been the hottest of the summer. Lin Duoduo had followed Wan the agent through the revolving glass door and into the spacious lobby of the Ya'an Apartments on East Third Ring Road. Outside it was unbearably hot, but inside the lobby it was cool and peaceful. She sat on a sofa while Wan walked over to reception to make a phone call. The elevators opened with a melodious "ping" and a lady in a cashmere dress and high heels emerged from the deep inner recesses of the lobby and walked past Lin Duoduo to the main entrance. She vanished through the revolving door, dissolving into the cruel summer outside.

A cleaning woman then appeared noiselessly beside Wan, silently mopping up Wan's reflection on the glossy smooth marble floor. The cleaner pursued Wan's footprints all the way back to the main entrance, then turned and followed Lin Duoduo's footprints right up to where she was sitting.

Without thinking, Lin Duoduo moved her backpack so that the side saying "Foreign Languages Academy" was facing the cleaner, then she straightened up and returned her gaze to the deep cave-like recesses of the lobby. Wan now came walking over to Lin Duoduo with a carefree smile on his face: "Unfortunately the client is not at home today, but I called her and she said there's no need for an interview: you've got the job."

That was the first time Lin Duoduo had been to the East Third Ring Road, and the first time she had set foot inside a luxury apartment building. It was a long way from her campus at Zhongguancun, and she had to take three different buses to get there. What struck her most was not so much the distance but the total separation between this world and her own.

Now, while Du Juan was rattling on beside her, trying to drum up support for her scheme, all Lin Duoduo could think of was that image of the cleaning woman, silently advancing with her mop, mechanically wiping away all the dust from the world outside. But then what? There would always be another person coming in to make the floor dirty. She felt Du Juan's scheme was as futile as that cleaner's job. She was the only one who could sit in the lobby of life and observe how futile it all was. Do you really think your petty scribbling will achieve anything? Will your cutting and pasting really create an ideal life for you? What is an ideal life anyway? Lin Duoduo felt that even being able to ask such questions made her more complex than Du Juan. The corners of her mouth and eyes inevitably revealed a fatalistic, skeptical, languid smile.

Lin Duoduo's smile made Du Juan really mad, because clearly she had changed, but Du Juan had no idea what was behind it all. She tried a new line of attack: "Hey Duoduo, I heard you didn't go home this summer?"

"Mmm."

"So you stayed in the dorm all by yourself?"

Lin Duoduo's mouth tensed up. It was her turn to be irritated.

Sensing that she was gaining the upper hand, Du Juan went straight for the jugular: "I heard Li Hao's wife had a baby."

"What's that got to do with me?" Lin Duoduo was blushing. Finally Du Juan had got her to lose her cool.

Li Hao was one of the more dynamic young lecturers in the department. The previous semester, someone had spotted Lin Duoduo and Li Hao watching a movie together at the cinema, sitting in the lovers' box seats. At that time Li Hao's pregnant wife had already gone back to her mother's to prepare for the delivery.

When did she come back? Lin thought. Was it during the summer or after the break?

"What's eating you?" Du Juan asked. "I was only thinking we should go over to their place and congratulate them on behalf of our class. Li Hao has always been good to our class, especially last semester when he helped us so much with staging that play."

"You're the class rep. That's the kind of thing you need to worry about." Lin Duoduo realized she had lost it just now and was trying her best to explain why she had said "What's that got to do with me?"

"Okay, wait till I've called them; you'll come along when I've arranged things, won't you?"

This was something she could agree to. Why not? Even though Li Hao had broken her heart and made her life hell this summer, now she was a worldly woman, and she should be able to just put all those feelings aside. So with a casual air, she enthusiastically replied: "Sounds great!" Such a positive response left Du Juan feeling quite startled. Just then, Lin Duoduo finally reached the service desk. She fished out her ID card from her satchel and pushed it through the service window along with the wire transfer receipt. The postal worker seated on the other side took one look, then impassively threw the receipt and card back out again: "You have to bring your own ID card."

Lin Duoduo stared back at her and for a moment looked as stunned as a wooden chicken. Luckily Du Juan's reactions were quicker, and she grabbed the ID card and receipt and pulled Lin Duoduo's arm. They had to push their way through the crowd but finally managed to stagger outside.

"What's all this then?" Du Juan asked, once they were safely in the square outside the post office. She was turning the suspicious ID card over in her hands, studying it carefully. It was definitely Lin Duoduo's photo on the card, but the name given was "Xu Yawen," and according to her date of birth, she was eight years older than Lin Duoduo.

Lin Duoduo looked mortified as she admitted, "I got a fake ID card."

"That's pretty obvious!" Du Juan replied, looking excited, "But why? Was it just for a lark?"

"I sat the IELTS exam for someone," Lin Duoduo said, blushing.

"Phew! Just now I thought it was something serious!" Du Juan exclaimed, relaxing: "I thought you had eloped with a guy, or something!" She made it sound like nothing had happened, but inside she was exultant. Finally she had rooted out Lin Duoduo's little secret!

Lin Duoduo was surprised: "You think this is no big deal?"

"What's the big fuss about taking a test for someone?" Du Juan replied. "Still, it is illegal to use a fake ID You're so careless—you should have destroyed it a long time ago."

Lin Duoduo knew that, but Wan had reminded her several times not to lose the ID as he definitely wanted it back. Several days ago he had called and told her he was coming over to get it. But you could never be sure when Wan would appear. He was never able to stick to an exact time. So Lin Duoduo had to carry the fake ID all that time. She had no idea why just now some little gremlin had caused her to take out that card instead of hers. How typical that Du Juan would be right beside her when she did it!

"Let's go back to the dorm," Du Juan said, walking off in front with a self-satisfied air. "We can have a good chat on the way."

Lin Duoduo followed reluctantly, still looking back at the post office.

When they got back to the dorm, Du Juan asked their classmate Liu Yinyin to go next door and get a few more people. When all the girls arrived, Du Juan opened her backpack and ceremoniously took out a plastic bag. She spread a newspaper on the table and emptied the contents, several official-looking seals, out of the plastic bag onto it. Everyone went "Wah!" and crowded around to admire them. So this is what they looked like!

Du Juan pointed at the seals one by one and explained the function of each: this was the signature seal of the university president; this was the official stamp of the government's education department; and this one was the "approved" stamp from their university department. Liu Yinyin wanted to pick up one of them to have a closer look, but after stretching out her hand she paused and asked: "Do I need to wear gloves?" Everyone burst out laughing at this, except for Du Juan, who replied with a serious face: "Don't worry, just pick it up."

Several girls who were standing closest each picked up a seal and took a careful look at it. These seals had clearly been used many times, so they were somewhat worn down, just like genuine seals would be. But apart from that, nobody could see anything very special about them. Du Juan explained: "Nowadays you can find people carving fake seals everywhere. But there's a big risk when you carve a new one. These seals have already stood the test of time. I heard last year one American university sent a forged transcript back to our school asking them to confirm its authenticity. Our registrar's office compared the forged version with their official records and found that the numbers didn't match up. But when they examined the seal imprint on the form, it looked completely genuine. If the seal was genuine, they reasoned, it must be because a student had found a loophole in their reporting procedure, and this was evidence of their own negligence. They certainly didn't want to admit they had been negligent, so they sent a reply to the American university telling them it was an authentic transcript!"

Not wanting to leave the task half finished, the classmates had a quick dinner and then got to work. Altering transcripts essentially meant increasing the percentages on the subjects for which they had received low marks, but because the reports were written by hand, they had to ensure that the handwriting remained completely consistent. It wouldn't do to have two different styles of handwriting on a single transcript. Their solution was to photocopy each report first, then take the copy and cut out the higher marks from their best subjects and paste them carefully over the lower marks on the original. Once this was done, they would take these altered reports to a photocopy shop and copy them to hide the changes. Finally they would stamp them with the forged seals to make them look completely genuine.

This work was quite tedious, so while they got on with it they kept each other entertained with all kinds of anecdotes and gossip. Only Lin Duoduo seemed preoccupied and out of sorts. Her GPA was already so high that there wasn't much point increasing it further. But the incident with the ID card had disturbed her and deflated all her former pride. The only reason she was helping out with the grade altering was to demonstrate solidarity with her classmates.

She had tried several times to make eye contact with Du Juan, hoping she could patch things up with her, but Du Juan steadfastly refused to look at her. That was because Du Juan's mind had already floated away to the male dorms. The top student in their class was a male student whose grades were even better than Lin Duoduo's. She was wondering whether that student would join their scheme, and whether he would be any good at it, since it was a very intricate task, a bit like doing fine embroidery. As for Lin Duoduo, Du Juan now knew she was no longer a threat, and she no longer had to pay any attention to her.

Lin Duoduo sensed the change in Du Juan's attitude, and felt somehow she had lost out.

Just after nine PM, Lin Duoduo's pager suddenly beeped. According to Wan, their client had lent this pager to her because "She's worried the test center might try to contact her, and if she can't understand their English, they will smell a rat." But no officials from the test center had contacted Lin Duoduo, and in fact the only times it beeped was when Wan wanted to meet her.

Each time they met up, he would have an English letter that "Xu Yawen" needed to be polished, or an English form that "Xu Yawen" had to fill in. The letters were being sent to all sorts of places: the Canadian immigration department, some college in England, even a zoo in South Africa. Wan said this was part of their "after-sales service." Once he even asked her to help the client complete an application to an online overseas matchmaking service. But since the start of the new semester, the pager had beeped only once: that was the time Wan had told Lin Duoduo he was coming to retrieve the fake ID card. None of her classmates had heard it beeping that time.

It was still unusual for students to have pagers, so when Lin Duoduo's pager suddenly beeped, her classmates were surprised. Holding the pager tightly in her hand, as if it was a grenade that might go off at any time if she loosened her grip, she scurried out of the dorm, followed by the curious gazes of all her classmates.

She ran downstairs, but seven or eight students were lined up waiting to use the only public phone in the dormitory. She went outside and hurried over to the convenience store, which had a payphone, but as luck would have it the phone was out of order. She would have to go off campus to find one.

Lin Duoduo's university was unique in that half the student body consisted of students from various foreign countries who had come to Beijing to study Chinese. The concentration of foreign students had in turn attracted a diverse collection of foreign-themed restaurants and bars outside the campus gates, with their signs displaying a mix of English, French, Japanese, and Korean. As soon as evening came, the sounds of numerous different languages would mix together on the street. Some local residents complained they now felt like foreigners in their own land, but other more trendy locals came there just to enjoy the cosmopolitan atmosphere.

During the summer, Lin Duoduo and Wan had always held their meetings in one of these bars called the Hawaii. After Lin Duoduo's pager sounded, she would take a book with her to the Hawaii, borrow the phone at their front desk to tell Wan she was there, then sit and read for half an hour or so until Wan turned up.

Strangely, though, the Hawaii seemed to have disappeared.

Instead she walked up the street and found some battered, card-operated pay phones under red mushroom shelters by the sidewalk. She selected a phone that appeared to be in working order and confirmed the phone number on the pager by the light of a street lamp. It was not the number Wan normally used.

She dialed the number, and a slightly brusque male voice answered: "Hello?"

Lin Duoduo asked: "Did somebody page me just now?"

The guy on the other end was silent for a moment, then asked: "Hugh are you?"

Hearing this strange accent, Lin Duoduo guessed he was a foreigner. Without pausing to think, she continued in English: "I was just wondering who paged my number, 15984?"

The man was delighted: "Ah yes, is that Miss Shhh?"

Warning bells suddenly sounded in Lin Duoduo's brain: *Damn!—it's the test center doing an investigation!"* she thought. But then, on reflection, she realized that no one would be doing investigations on a Saturday evening: surely they wouldn't be that conscientious! Despite this, she still felt agitated, so much so that she forgot her fake identity's full name: "Yes, this is, er, Miss Xu," she replied.

The caller exclaimed enthusiastically: "Is it okay if I call you that then: Shhh?"

"No problem," she answered. "And you are?"

"Robert. I just arrived in Beijing."

"Hi Robert. Which Robert are you again?"

"Robert Diaz, from Louisiana. Shhh—Yaaah—When . . . Did I say it right?"

"That's right, Xu Yawen. This is such a surprise!" Lin Duoduo was still trying to work out what this phone call from out of the blue was all about.

"I sent you an email: didn't you receive it?"

"I have several email accounts: which one did you send it to?"

The caller gave the name of a matchmaking website: Women Seeking Men.

Finally Lin Duoduo understood. This must be a man Xu Yawen had chosen online.

"Can we meet up?" Robert asked. He did have quite a pleasant voice.

"I . . ." Lin Duoduo hesitated. "Let me think about it." Then she hung up without saying another word.

But what was there to think about? And how would she go about thinking about it? Lin Duoduo had no idea. She just felt it would be inappropriate to take it any further. But exactly how was it inappropriate? Would it be appropriate instead for her to go all the way back to the Ya'an Apartments and find this "Xu Yawen," whom she had never even met, and tell her: "Robert from Louisiana is here for a blind date

65

with you"? Put another way, if she really was "Xu Yawen," would it be appropriate for her to go and see this Robert?

Feeling unsettled, Lin Duoduo headed back to campus. Ironically, on her way back she spotted the Hawaii bar— typical, now that she didn't need to find it. The owner had renovated the place, blocking off the main door that faced the road, and opening a new door in a small alleyway at the side. Above the alleyway entrance, hanging down above peoples' heads was a line of little red lanterns tied to a rope. Each lantern had one English letter on it, and together they spelled the name "H-a-w-a-i-i."

"I'll think about it," Lin Duoduo repeated to herself.

As she walked through the main campus gate lost in her thoughts, the gate warden came running out of the lodge and blocked her way forward, demanding her student ID Of course, in her haste to make the call just now, Lin Duoduo had forgotten to bring her ID card. She told the warden: "I just came out a few minutes ago." But the warden said: "It's not my job to watch people going out: my job is to watch them going in!"

"So what am I supposed to do, then?" asked Lin Duoduo.

"You'll have to call your class counselor to vouch for you," the warden replied, "Or your class rep will do."

"In that case, I won't come in today," Lin Duoduo snorted. "Stick that up your pipe and smoke it!"

When Lin Duoduo failed to return that night, Du Juan was quite surprised. She thought she had uncovered Lin Duoduo's secrets, but apparently there were still deeper mysteries yet to be revealed. The next day was Sunday, and all the other girls in the dorm took their altered grade reports to be photocopied, but Du Juan was too worried to go with them. Sunday evening, Lin Duoduo still hadn't returned, and she failed to show up for Monday's political economy class as well. When the teacher called Lin Duoduo's name on the roll, Du Juan answered "here!" on her behalf (there were so many students in the class that the teacher didn't notice).

On Monday evening, as she looked at Lin Duoduo's empty bed, Du Juan began to feel the situation was getting serious. She decided if there were no sign of Lin Duoduo by Tuesday lunchtime, she would report her absence to the department office.

On Tuesdays at ten AM they had World Literature. This was a so-called easy credit class. By their fourth year, some students whose grade point average was low would select a class that was painless, one where just turning up with their ears working would be more or less enough to get them at least an eighty percent. Usually these kinds of classes were taught by teachers who were bland but approachable, teachers who understood what the students were after. But this year World Literature was being taught by Li Hao.

Li Hao's star was rising: he had just published a new book and been interviewed on television several times, not to mention that his wife had delivered a baby girl. He was riding on the crest of a wave of success. Full of self-confidence, on the first day of class he stood at the raised lectern, and in a resounding, pompous voice, as if he was in charge of the whole world, he declared: "Students: I know it's not convenient for you to take this class in your final year. Some of you are sitting the graduate admissions exams; some of you are planning to go overseas, taking the TOEFL test, the GRE, doing your graduation thesis, etc. There may be some who really want to gain a deeper understanding of World Literature, especially literature that is not written in English, but those students are surely in the minority! Some of you might say, Professor, why don't you just tell us a bunch of interesting anecdotes about literary history, and then mark our exams with one eye open and one eye closed. That way we can all relax. But I do not wish to do that! Because I believe that what I am going to teach you has value and will nourish you. For this reason, I plan to be even stricter in teaching this class and marking your assignments than I would be for a first year class. Today I am releasing this warning shot across the bow to preempt you from complaining about my strictness later on!"

He had just completed this spiel when Lin Duoduo appeared in the doorway. Li Hao turned his head and saw Lin Duoduo. Though it was a large lecture hall, it was as if they had just encountered each other on a narrow path. For an instant, Li Hao looked flustered, then immediately covered it up by focusing all his attention on the attendance list.

"You're late, young lady," Li Hao said. "What's your name?"

"Just choose any name!" Lin Duoduo replied coldly.

This caused students to start whispering to each other, and Li Hao clearly felt extremely embarrassed. Still not daring to look Lin Duoduo in the eye, he pretended to be unruffled and instead addressed the hundred or so students seated in the hall: "Would the class rep of this class come and speak to me after the lecture."

Du Juan, who was sitting in the back row, immediately raised her hand and called out: "No problem!"

Lin Duoduo looked over and saw there was an empty seat next to Du Juan, so she sauntered up the steps all the way to the back row. Du Juan stood to let her through, and she unconsciously leaned back as Lin Duoduo squeezed past, as if trying to avoid her.

A pungent, strange and unpleasant odor emanated from Lin Duoduo's body.

"You just came straight here without going back to the dorm?" Du Juan whispered after Lin Duoduo sat down.

"Mmm," Lin Duoduo murmured casually. She was still wearing the same clothes she had on two days earlier when she had disappeared without warning, and she had an unwashed and disheveled appearance. She had also come empty-handed, without any pens, paper, or textbook.

Du Juan took out a pen and tore off a few sheets of paper from her notebook, giving them to Lin Duoduo: "We'd better listen to the lecture."

After class, Lin Duoduo devoured a huge lunch in the cafeteria, then went back to the dorm and lay on her bed. A mosquito net hung down over each student's bed. It was designed to prevent them from getting bitten in the summer, but most students used it throughout the year as a kind of privacy screen when they didn't want to be disturbed by their roommates. As soon as Lin Duoduo lay down behind her net, she fell into a deep sleep. For the past three nights, she had been shacked up with Robert in his hotel, and she was completely exhausted.

She slept like a log all the rest of the day. The whole afternoon, her roommates came and went in the dorm room, but nothing stirred her. Du Juan still hadn't got around to photocopying her altered grade reports, but now she saw Lin Duoduo sleeping soundly in her bed, she felt more at ease and after lunch she went off to make the copies.

That evening, all the girls gathered in the dorm room

to fix the "official seals" on the reports. First they affixed their departmental office seal, then, after folding the reports, they slipped them into envelopes, sealed the envelopes and stamped them over the flaps with the university president's signature seal. This was a very easy job which didn't require much concentration, so they chatted and joked with each other as they did it. Someone raised the subject of Lin Duoduo, but Du Juan pointed at Lin Duoduo's bed and said: "Shhh!" Only then did the person realize that Lin Duoduo was actually there sleeping in the dorm room, and changed the subject.

But in her dreams, Lin Duoduo heard that light wispy sound "Shhh!" She opened her eyes and saw Robert standing naked in front of her, just a couple of feet away. "What are you doing here?" she asked. "You have to leave now!" She sat up and grabbed her dress, trying to cover her naked body. Robert was smiling indulgently, and he pulled the dress down to reveal her nakedness again. In the dark room, they wrestled with the dress. Robert then called her "Shhh!" She was irritated and replied: "I'm not Xu, I'm Lin."

Robert's smile floated before her: "Shhhh . . . !"

He had never quite managed to pronounce Xu properly, no matter how many times Lin Duoduo taught him. He just didn't seem to be able to curl up his lips like a Chinese person and create that short vowel, something between an "eee" and an "uuu." Once he curled up his lips they stayed curled, blocking any vowels from getting out at all.

"I am Lin . . ." Lin Duoduo was trying to say.

Robert put his finger on her lips and said: "Shhh . . ."

In her dream, Lin Duoduo felt she was being dragged away from her classmates in the dorm room and down into a bottomless pit . . . she was about to be humiliated in front of them. All the time her pager was insistently beeping.

Robert suddenly disappeared, and she saw Du Juan outside her mosquito net, stamping a seal on an envelope. She probably hadn't got it right the first time, so she was inking the seal again in the ink tin, and then she used both hands to stamp it down violently on the envelope with a dull thud.

Lin Duoduo sat up and realized she was still wearing her clothes. Not only that, but they were the same clothes she had worn for three days, emitting their acrid stink of body odor. She got out her pager and saw that Wan had called her. Lifting up the mosquito net, she tidied her clothes and brushed her hair, then, ignoring the stares of all her roommates, she walked straight out of the dorm.

As soon as the door closed behind her, everyone started arguing vociferously about why she was behaving so outrageously, but no one seemed to know exactly what kind of trouble she was in.

Lin Duoduo went downstairs. As usual there was an enormous lineup waiting for the dorm lodge telephone. She decided to head for the Hawaii and call Wan from there, but surprisingly when she stepped outside she saw Wan chatting to another student across the street. She waited inconspicuously until that student went off, then walked over and greeted Wan: "I see business is good!" she said.

Wan was a forty-something Beijing-born-and-bred local. Though he didn't have any formal qualifications, he had a quick mind.

"Not too bad," he laughed. "I just came to collect that ID card from you."

Lin Duoduo handed him the ID and the pager.

"You can keep the pager: the client has already gone

overseas and she doesn't need it back."

"It's not much use to me," replied Lin Duoduo.

"Keep it just in case I need to contact you again. I have another job coming up soon, a professional competency test."

Lin Duoduo reflected for a moment, then took back the pager.

The lights were turned off in all the dorms at ten PM. Lin Duoduo had just returned to her dorm room when it went dark. All her roommates were lying in their beds still chatting away. Before this they had basically been well-behaved students who followed all the rules, and changing their grade reports was their first major transgression. They found it all wonderfully exciting.

Though the lights were off in the dorm rooms, the power was still on in the communal bathroom. Lin Duoduo collected her washbasin from under the bed and tiptoed out to have a shower. Half an hour later, she tiptoed back again, quietly put away her things, and silently slipped into bed behind her mosquito net. Everyone was still making a big racket, competing for bragging rights, until Du Juan finally cut them off: "Look, can't you keep your mouths shut? It's not like we've done anything to be proud of."

Liu Yinyin imitated Du Juan's voice: "I'll tell you one more time: do not tell anyone about this— not your parents, not your boyfriends, and if you have any children in the future, don't tell them either!"

A burst of laughter rang out in the dorm room, then in the darkness one girl asked: "Why can't I tell my children? I want to give them a traditional education. I plan to tell them: your old mother had to suffer a lot and use all her cunning strategies so that you could be born in America."

Another voice replied: "I don't think you should tell them. You don't want to besmirch your glorious image in their eyes."

"Hmph! If my children dare to disrespect me, I'll send them right back to China!" Liu Yinyin exclaimed.

"That's enough," said Du Juan. "Shut your mouths and go to sleep!"

The dorm grew quiet, and in the darkness Lin Duoduo felt at peace as she smelled the fragrance of cheap soap on her body. Though she still sensed a huge empty hole in her heart, through which a sharp wind was howling, at least her body had returned to her dorm and was wrapped snugly in her own bed behind her own mosquito net, in the calm eye of the storm.

Lin Duoduo gradually got back into her usual routine, but she didn't talk much to her classmates anymore. Her classmates didn't consciously exclude her or avoid her, but they didn't want to intrude on her space, and somehow a screen seemed to have formed around her. During lunchtime the next Saturday, Du Juan saw Lin Duoduo sitting all alone in the cafeteria and, taking the initiative, went over to her.

"Duoduo, did you manage to cash that wire transfer yet?"

"Not yet."

"I'll get it for you, if you like."

"I thought only the recipient could pick it up."

"You can authorize someone else to do it. Your agent just needs to show your ID card and her own ID. I wouldn't recommend you going to pick it up yourself in case it's the same postal worker and she recognizes you. Then you'd be in trouble."

Lin Duoduo took the wire transfer receipt and her ID

card out of her bag. She had kept these on her ever since that day, and on several occasions when she passed the post office she had wondered whether to try her luck, but just like Du Juan said, she was afraid the postal worker would recognize her.

Du Juan took the card and receipt and put them in her own bag, then added: "Oh yes: this afternoon the male students are going to change their grade reports, and I wanted to find two people to go over and help. Can you make it?"

"Ok," Lin Duoduo replied. She didn't sound irritated, but neither was she enthusiastic.

"As far as I recall, you never changed your grades, did you? Since we still have the seals, why don't you do yours this afternoon as well?" Du Juan then winked at Lin Duoduo: "These seals will soon have to be passed on to the next generation!"

Lin Duoduo gave a weak laugh.

Du Juan noticed that Lin Duoduo was gnawing at a pork rib: "Does your family still live in a log house?"

"Whatever made you think that?"

Du Juan smiled smugly. She had done a little investigating and found out that Lin Duoduo was a member of the Dong ethnic group.

"I'm planning to get some friends together and visit Guilin over the winter break. Is that far from your home?"

"It's not that far," Lin Duoduo replied, her mouth twitching slightly, "But I don't want to go home."

"Why not?"

Lin Duoduo chewed for a bit, then spat the rib bone onto the table: "My mom got really sick during the summer, and I was supposed to stay and look after her, but someone called me and I foolishly came back to Beijing. Now my mom's dead and the rest of my family are all mad at me."

"Was it that bald-headed middle-aged guy?" When Lin Duoduo had gone downstairs to return the pager, the scene outside the dorm building had been witnessed by all her roommates from the window of the dorm room. She thought Wan looked fine, but she hadn't noticed his bald patch—it must have been visible from upstairs.

"You mean Wan? No, the whole test-taking thing was after that."

"So who was it?"

"That's enough," Lin Duoduo said, frowning. "Don't think I have to tell you everything just because you're helping collect my money!"

"Okay, but I'm not doing it for nothing!" Du Juan shot back. "You at least owe me a bottle of yogurt!"

"Okay."

"No actually, make that a bottle of yogurt for each girl in our class."

"Okay, Okay!"

That Sunday evening, several classmates went with Lin Duoduo to the shopping mall to help her spend some of her money. The closest shopping district to the campus was at the Elm Tree intersection. Four big malls, China Friend, Contemporary, Friendship, and Tranquility, squatted on the four corners of the intersection, facing each other. One thing the girls liked to do a lot was to shop in small street markets where they could bargain back and forth as much as they liked. They rarely came to these fancy high-class department stores, and when they did it was only in a big group so they could give each other moral support when faced with the snobby salespeople.

But after window-shopping through three of the four malls, they hadn't been particularly dazzled. They just felt dazed by the fact that all the malls and their products were pretty much identical, and all of them were extremely expensive. Was this what all the fuss was about? Their faces started to display the expression of people who have seen it all and were no longer impressed by any of it.

But Lin Duoduo still had a flash of determined resolution in her eyes. She was looking to buy a gray cashmere skirt, and she firmly believed that if she just kept on searching through those racks of generic looking clothes, she would surely find a unique skirt that would satisfy all her requirements. Her hard work and determination were finally rewarded when in the fourth mall she discovered a light gray knitted dress. Though the design and material were not absolutely perfect, they were close enough to get her excited.

Initially her friends criticized her choice. They said the dress looked old-fashioned, not the kind of thing a young hip student would wear. "And what about the price?" they tutted disapprovingly. "Lin Duoduo, have you won the lottery or something?" But Lin Duoduo ignored them and went off by herself to the fitting room to try it on. When she came back out wearing it, the assembled girls couldn't help exclaiming "Wow!" It was just like the time Du Juan had pulled out those forged seals from her bag. Lin Duoduo had been transformed into a different person.

She paid for the dress, then borrowed some scissors from the shop assistant to cut off the labels and put her old clothes into the beautifully designed paper bag with the store's logo on it. Attended by her fellow student minions, Lin Duoduo left the mall feeling deeply satisfied. After they came out, Du Juan led them like fish strung on a line around the corner and into a cold beverage store. Lin Duoduo treated each and every one of them to a bottle of yogurt.

It was the next World Literature class, and just one minute before the bell sounded at the end of the lecture, Lin Duoduo casually strolled in. She was wearing the gray knitted form-fitting ultra mini skirt that she had recently purchased, with high heels and wearing her tea-colored shades forehead. She sauntered to the back row, her head held high, as if nobody else was in the room.

Du Juan was quite concerned about her get-up: it was one thing to wear that when you were out in the evening, but not when you were coming to class. Du Juan was someone who liked to have clear boundaries.

The lecturer, Li Hao, also looked discomfited by Lin Duoduo's outfit. He couldn't help gazing at her back for a moment, and only with some difficulty did he manage to pull himself together, refocus his eyes on a point in the middle distance, and get back to being a serious lecturer.

"Will the class rep come and see me at the end," he said.

After the bell rang, Lin Duoduo walked out past the lectern. Li Hao, who had been talking to Du Juan, the class rep, about her, called out: "Lin Duoduo, wait a moment."

All the other students drifted out in small groups, leaving just the three of them.

"What did you want?" asked Lin Duoduo.

"We need to discuss the topic of your graduation thesis," Li Hao said. "We're already a month into the term, and if you don't give me your topic you're going to miss the deadline."

Lin Duoduo suddenly remembered last semester, when they had chosen their thesis supervisor, she had selected Li Hao.

"I want to change supervisors," she said.

"Duoduo, it's a bit late to change now," Du Juan said.

"I don't care," Lin Duoduo replied with a shrug. "What's the worst thing that can happen? I miss the deadline and I don't get a degree? Big deal!" A mysterious languid smile was playing on Lin Duoduo's lips, and she was lightly tapping one of her pointed high heels on the ground, like someone who had seen through life's illusions.

"Not get your degree after spending four years in college? You'll surely regret that in the future," Li Hao said.

"Teacher, is that the best you can do to persuade me?"

Li Hao was momentarily lost for words. Just then, Lin Duoduo's pager beeped. She made a big show of fishing it out of her bag and looking at it: "See, I can make money already without having a degree!"

"Duoduo . . ." Du Juan said.

"Just leave it," Lin Duoduo said scornfully. "Do you really think you're any better than me?"

Du Juan blushed scarlet.

"See you later," Lin Duoduo said, then turned and walked out.

Du Juan ran after her: "Duoduo, don't go. Listen to me first. I know you look down on me, and we've all done some bad things." She was holding onto Lin Duoduo's arm. Lin Duoduo tried to make her release her grip, but Du Juan seemed to be hanging on for dear life. Lin Duoduo had no choice but to stand still.

"Duoduo," continued Du Juan, releasing her arm and cupping her hands in front of her own chest, as if she was about to take out her heart and show it to Lin Duoduo: "No matter how many bad things you do, you have to be clear in your heart: they are just means to an end, that's all. You mustn't lose yourself in your mistakes."

Lin Duoduo moved the sunglasses down from her forehead, covering her eyes. She looked really cool. "Are you saying I'm already lost? Well, so what if I am?"

"I'm worried you won't be able to turn back again," said Du Juan.

Lin Duoduo turned and walked off, and sure enough, she didn't look back.

"Duoduo!" Du Juan shouted.

With her hips swaying slightly, trying to look calm and collected, Lin Duoduo walked out of the lecture building. But as soon as she reached the asphalt path outside, she stretched out her legs and sprinted off, like a bird startled by a gunshot.

"Duoduo!" Du Juan kept shouting till her voice went hoarse.

Lin Duoduo kept on running, as if fleeing from herself.

From then on, Duoduo developed the habit of running everywhere. Wherever she went, she always seemed to be in a great rush. On campus, people would only catch a glimpse of her as she rushed past, sometimes on the main road between the classrooms and the library, other times on the small path from the departmental office to the dorm building. On many occasions, as she rushed about, she was wearing that knitted, form-fitting ultra mini skirt. People who spotted her couldn't help turning back for another look, especially the male students, who were concerned that her skirt might suddenly rip open. As she continued rushing around, those who knew her no longer felt it was strange, and those who didn't know her, seeing her for the first time running by in her ultra mini skirt, just assumed she was a foreign student from Japan or South Korea or Singapore.

Foreigners were pretty weird after all.

But in her dreams, she always seemed to be running too slowly. In her dreams she was an eraser, flying back in time, rubbing out everything that had happened in her life. All the places she had ever visited were sketched on a crumpled piece of paper: the convenience store by the university gate, the string of red lanterns spelling the name Hawaii Restaurant, the four shopping malls at the Elm Tree intersection . . . the drawings of all those places were rubbed out, leaving no traces.

But each time she rubbed something out, she lost a part of herself too, because she was the eraser.

It was really tiring having this dream; every time she changed to a different scene it took a new effort of will to keep it going. If she didn't wake up soon, she would inevitably travel along the East Third Ring Road past the Ya'an Apartments . . . The longest and most difficult part of her dream was when she reached Beijing Station and took a train all the way south, finally arriving at a fairytale scene of clear mountains, pure waters, and luxuriant forests. In her dream she told herself: *This is the end of the paper scroll; you won't ever come this far again. Your grimy body has already been reduced to countless tiny flakes of rubber. If you go any further, nothing will be left of you.* But why was she so reluctant to wake up even now? It's because just then, on the horizon, she saw the beautiful, pure light of a new dawn of innocence.

A SLICE OF GINGER

IN THE WHOLE WIDE WORLD THERE'S SURELY NO WOMAN who doesn't want to be more beautiful than everyone else—especially when that woman is someone like me, who has to rely on her looks to try and get ahead. I'm twenty-five with no college degree or special qualifications, and the main reason I moved from Beijing to Hainan Island is that I heard good looks are a valuable asset here. So I'd never want anyone else to have more of that resource than me, would I?

But last night, that was exactly what I desperately found myself wanting.

I came to Hainan a month ago. Before I got here, a friend had given me an introduction to Mr. Guan, telling me to go see him as soon as I got off the plane. A few years earlier, Mr. Guan's company had been right in the thick of things in the Hainan business world, but when the local economy tanked, the company moved its headquarters back to the mainland and only kept a small branch office here on the island. Mr. Guan was the branch office director. Though I'd heard of the recession that had hit Hainan, I was still full of grand ambitions, and I thought of this first job as merely a stepping-stone to greater things. But when I actually saw the Hainan streets so empty of life I realized how lucky I was to have even this small opportunity. Though my salary was pretty low, the branch office did have its own piece of real estate which doubled as both workplace and staff residence. As long as Mr. Guan took me on, I would at least have a place to shelter from the wind and rain.

Luckily, Mr. Guan did take me on, something which gave me renewed respect for my friend's persuasive powers.

But Mr. Guan didn't really know me, and he was pretty cautious at first. Sometimes when we were chatting, he would use some local Hainan anecdotes to make insinuations. One of these was about how Hainan girls loved to find an easy job in a company to pay the bills, but then they would spend every night working as escorts in bars and nightclubs seeking to double their salaries. Mr. Guan was probably just trying to give me an advance warning, but the effect on me was completely the opposite: it made me even more curious about the lives of those so-called "escort girls."

Mind you, that was all just background to the main story. You'll never guess what happened to me last night.

At six PM I was just about to leave work when suddenly the power went off in the office. In Hainan, sudden power cuts are a frequent occurrence, and nobody was surprised by this one. It just made the office more peaceful for a moment. Everyone sat there sunk in their own thoughts, wondering how they were going to entertain themselves that evening. As for me, I was regretting the long nap I'd taken after lunch, which made me feel particularly alert in the darkness. In this silence, which dragged on unpredictably, I keenly felt a sense of time wasted: during the day, it was wasted by my sleep, and tonight it would be wasted by my insomnia.

But right then the phone rang. Mr. Guan answered it, and the red "line busy" light blinked on and off in the darkness. It was always fascinating to observe Mr. Guan's body language when he was on the phone, so I turned round and watched him from a distance.

"Hello, Phnom Penh Trading. Yes, this is Guan. May I ask who's calling? . . .

"You what? You want me to guess?" Mr. Guan looked up for a moment, as if asking Heaven for assistance. "Mr. Chen? It's got to be Director Chen!" Mr. Guan lowered his head again, looking deeply sincere. "Are you really gracing Hainan with your presence? Just wait there, Director Chen, I'll come over right away."

After hanging up, Mr. Guan's eyes met mine for a second. With a delighted expression, he said to me: "Linda, let's go: I'll buy you dinner." I replied: "No way! Hainan is way too complicated for me: what'll I do if you go and sell me off to some night club?" But Mr. Guan pretended he hadn't heard me and strode off to the next room to change into his business suit.

I didn't want to ruffle his feathers too much, so I stood up and got ready to go out with him. But I knew the real reason he was inviting me to dinner was to get me to drink wine so he wouldn't have to. I'm a pretty good drinker, and when he had to deal with a guest who was into drinking contests, he liked to enlist me to hold up his end of the table.

In actual fact I don't have a great capacity for drink, but I just did it because I felt I had no choice. My position in the company was not that secure, so I took every opportunity to show off my meager talent—even if it was just my drinking talent.

I'm pretty sure Mr. Guan was aware of this.

Once we were in the car, Mr. Guan got very excited, as if the God of Wealth was about to pay him a visit. He asked the driver: "What's the price of gasoline in Hainan?" The driver gave him a number, and Mr. Guan muttered to himself: "Yep, it's doable." It was then I realized this Manager Chen must be the guy Mr. Guan was always rattling on about: Chen Xinzhang, the Oil King.

We met Chen Xinzhang in a Northern Chinese-style restaurant downtown. He was sitting at a six-person round table with a tall tough-looking young guy. On the table were three bottles of Erguotou brand liquor and some fried snacks.

Mr. Guan loved to tell anecdotes about Chen Xinzhang, especially how he really became somebody when he managed to corner the Hainan oil market. Most of the time Chen kept a pretty low profile, and when he visited Hainan, he would do his best to avoid the limelight, hiding out like a pop star avoiding his fans. But everything changed if he had a drink. A few shots of liquor, and he was like a different man, totally indiscreet, randomly calling his contacts to see if they would do him a favor and pick up the tab. Whoever got his call would feel like fortune was finally smiling on them, and today it just happened to be Mr. Guan. But I noticed when Mr. Guan sat down he kept glancing at the two empty seats at the table. I guessed he felt uneasy, worried that Chen Xinzhang would get carried away and invite some more friends to compete for his attention.

This Chen Xinzhang was skinny, not very tall, and looked like a pretty straightforward type. Once we were seated, he immediately filled Mr. Guan's glass with liquor and told him to drink it as a punishment for being late. Mr. Guan drank it down as he explained: "Every day I was longing for you to visit, but nobody told me it would be today. Next time if you can just let me know in advance, I'll come and meet you at the airport."

Chen Xinzhang smiled but didn't respond. Mr. Guan then turned to the young guy, who was probably his bodyguard: "How about you act as my secret lookout, bro? Next time Director Chen's on his way to Hainan, give me a heads up, okay?" Hearing Mr. Guan address the bodyguard as "bro" set my teeth on edge: after all, Mr. Guan came from an educated background, and it felt incongruous to hear him using ghetto language.

But the bodyguard didn't seem to mind. He grinned like an idiot, and replied: "No problem, bro—let's drink a toast to it!"

So once more Mr. Guan's glass was filled to the brim.

Mr. Guan said: "That's my limit. I'll throw in the towel now and Linda can drink with you instead." This was his way of introducing me into the fray. I was just about to pick up his wine glass and drink when a hand which turned out to be Chen Xinzhang's took away the glass. He laughingly teased Mr. Guan: "You can't give her your glass! When drinking, there are certain rules you have to follow."

He then got a clean glass, filled it, and placed it in front of me. I downed it in one shot.

"Great!" said Chen Xinzhang. "I don't think we've been properly introduced."

Mr. Guan gave a start: "Sorry, I forgot to tell you. This is Linda."

"Ah, Linda." He looked me over for a while: "Why didn't I see you last time I was in Hainan?"

"I've only been here a month," I replied

"What's your impression of Hainan?"

I hesitated a moment—it was such a general question that I wasn't sure how to respond.

He tried another question: "So what are you doing here?

Hainan's too small a place for you to develop your full potential."

I laughed but didn't say anything.

He then turned to ask Mr. Guan: "How's business recently?"

Mr. Guan replied: "I was just going to give you a full report on that."

Chen Xinzhang waved him away: "What's with all the polite formalities: I'm not your boss, am I?"

Mr. Guan replied: "Of course I need to be polite: you're the Oil King. If you don't supply your oil, all the cars in Haikou will have to convert to natural gas!"

I couldn't suppress an audible giggle, but immediately realized this was not appropriate and quickly controlled myself. During these facial contortions, Chen Xinzhang gave me a look, then said to Mr. Guan: "I'll supply you with five hundred thousand."

"Five hundred thousand?" Mr. Guan's face was a picture of stupefaction. I guessed that this figure represented a huge amount: was it five hundred thousand liters . . . or tons? How did people measure oil anyway? I recalled the gasoline price that our driver had given earlier. Even if it was just liters, there was no way we could find that sort of cash up front. I thought I must have misunderstood something, but when I looked over at Mr. Guan, his face displayed exactly the kind of disbelief that I was feeling. And yet . . .

I'd heard many rumors of people making their fortunes overnight in Hainan. But up to now, these rumors hadn't had any real impact on me. They were inert, like unused firecrackers lying on the shelf of a discount store. But suddenly they started exploding in my brain, left right and center. Was it really Mr. Guan's turn to make it big now—

just because this Chen Xinzhang happened to get drunk and casually offer him five hundred thousand?

I glanced at Chen Xinzhang and found him looking at me.

"Linda," he asked: "You can really drink, can't you?"

"Of course, of course," insisted Mr. Guan, waking from his daze, "Linda can totally hold her wine."

So he filled my glass again and placed it in front of me. I didn't bother politely refusing, and drained it in one shot.

Chen Xinzhang couldn't take his eyes off the wineglass as I lifted it, tipped it back, poured the wine down my throat, then replaced the glass on the table. He then refocused his gaze from the glass to my face, and said: "I suggest you come back to Beijing and work for my company. You can be my second in command."

I looked over at Mr. Guan, not knowing what to say. Mr. Guan was even more stunned than I: "She's really not qualified . . ." But then he hesitated. He was obviously about to belittle me, but then he realized that saying I was useless wouldn't make him look good. After all, I was still one of his employees.

Still not sure how to proceed, I decided to adopt a please everybody strategy: "I do hope to return to Beijing at some point, and I'll definitely take you up on your kind offer. But for now, if you can just look after my boss, he's sure to give me a raise, and then I'll be more than happy!"

Mr. Guan laughed: "Well said, Linda!"

I acknowledged his compliment with a slight nod. I was feeling pretty pleased with myself. That was one of my quirks: whenever I made some witty remark, even if no one else appreciated it, I would be on top of the world for hours. No doubt this was the reason I had never succeeded in life. As soon as I started admiring myself, I would drop my guard, and I assumed everyone else would drop their guard as well, forgetting that the situation could change very rapidly.

This time was no different. Just when I was feeling really smug, Chen Xinzhang stretched out his hand, took the wine bottle and filled up my glass again. In my half-dazed, self-satisfied state, I somehow let myself down another three glasses, to the point where Chen Xinzhang said: "Okay, Linda, you might as well just finish off this bottle." At that point I finally snapped out of my stupor. I looked at the bottle, and saw that it was almost empty. *I could deal with that*, I thought, and steeled myself to drink one more glass. But then Chen Xinzhang gave a sly grin and pointed to an unopened bottle: "You really do have a deep capacity, Linda. I'll have to make sure your drinking urge is really satisfied tonight!" Realizing that I was losing ground in this skirmish, I forced myself to sober up a bit. I put down my glass and started to engage in witty banter.

When it came to witty banter, I wasn't just good at it, I was an outstanding competitor, and the more pressure I faced the more brilliantly I would distinguish myself. This time I said: Isn't it strange that when people eat dinner and drink wine, they can never avoid being defeated. But who are they really losing to? Only themselves, because they always end up saying "I can't eat any more" or "I've really had enough to drink." You never see people eating and drinking so much that the restaurant manager has to come out and apologize, saying: "Really sorry but we've run out of supplies: we'll have to ask you distinguished guests to leave." It's the same when we try to fight against time. No matter how talented we are, in the end we're all going to kick the bucket. There's no way we can force the god of time to come out and apologize, saying: "Sorry, I don't have any time left for you to live in, so please could you do me a favor and do yourselves in!" Don't you think that's pretty interesting, ha ha ha . . .

I laughed for a bit, but when I looked over at Mr. Guan, he didn't seem impressed, so I turned to Chen Xinzhang. He laughed and said: "Well, based on that, I can see Linda's had enough to drink!"

"Oh no, far from it," I hastily reassured him.

But Chen Xinzhang laughed again: "Let's get the check." Mr. Guan immediately waved his arm to call over the waitress, but Chen stopped him and stood up, heading toward the front. Mr. Guan got up as if to try and get there to pay first, but seeing Chen Xinzhang was not going to give way, he didn't force the issue.

As he watched Chen Xinzhang walking off, Mr. Guan whispered to me: "Linda, do you think this deal's really going to happen?" I knew he was always dreaming of making his fortune, and even though 500,000 was a totally unrealistic figure, he'd much rather believe it than not. Not surprising really, because in Hainan if you don't even dare to dream then what could you hope to achieve? I glanced at the bodyguard, who hadn't moved an inch, and guessed that he wasn't interested in our conversation, so I decided to humor Mr. Guan. "I'm sure it won't be a problem. You two are old friends, and both of you have strong and reputable companies."

I thought I was being very subtle by not even hinting at my own contribution, even though I'd forced down at least a half bottle of liquor, which surely deserved some gratitude. But Mr. Guan still couldn't seem to relax: "I just don't see why he had to insist on paying?"

Suddenly I understood: when he insisted on picking up the tab for the meal, Chen Xinzhang was indicating that he wanted something else from Mr. Guan. But what could that be?

Mr. Guan looked at me, but I didn't make eye contact. I realized that Chen Xinzhang was a pretty formidable opponent, and all my efforts had been in vain. All that stuff about female charm, sweet smiles and clever conversation—it might work back in Beijing, but it was useless in Hainan. Here you had to back up your words with action.

After a pregnant pause, Mr. Guan suggested: "We could at least invite him to go dancing." Seemed like he was almost begging me, but before I had a chance to refuse, Chen Xinzhang was back. Mr. Guan didn't waste any words, and the decision was made to go dancing. As the four of us left the restaurant and headed for the car, Mr. Guan surreptitiously tugged at my arm, as if trying to give me some kind of signal. But I didn't turn to look at him. I was sure his expression was just as perplexing as my own mood.

I knew I was starting to get into deep water. In the car, Chen Xinzhang seemed to be quite drunk already. He was rambling on about random topics, but two words kept recurring: one was "Linda" and the other was "five hundred thousand." As for Mr. Guan, he just sat there in silence. I was looking out the car window, really regretting my decision to come out with him this evening. But then I thought, *if I don't want to do it, who's going to force me? I can totally tell them to stop the car and let them watch me as I strut off into the sunset like a movie heroine.*

But then what? Mr. Guan would definitely be offended. Maybe he would fire me. Maybe I would end up on the streets. This put a damper on my mood. Suddenly my future prospects seemed bleak indeed. Of course, if I did decide to stay in Hainan, I could become an escort. Now there's an idea: an escort! The car was already on Haifu Road, so I suggested: "How about we try Flowery Immortals?"

Chen Xinzhang replied: "Okay, you're the boss."

The car drove on with everyone lost in their own thoughts. I was feeling agitated, but I pretended to be relaxed. I said in an innocent tone, "I've heard the escorts at Flowery Immortals are all really pretty; I've always wanted to see them for myself."

Chen Xinzhang said, "Do you often go nightclubbing?"

"This is the first time actually. If it wasn't for your visit, I can't imagine my boss would invite me!"

"So how do you know the girls at Flowery Immortals are pretty?"

I had to give a truthful answer: "It's true I've only heard it from other people, but there must be some truth to the rumors."

This probably sounded reasonable enough, and Chen Xinzhang didn't interrogate me any further. But as the car turned into the parking lot, for the first time in my life I had this thought: *Please let the girls in this dance club be delicate as jade and beautiful as fairies. As God is my witness, I promise not to feel even the slightest twinge of jealousy.*

Here I should give a bit of background. Ever since I can remember, I've always been extremely jealous of pretty girls. It's not that I'm jealous in other respects: there's plenty of girls who are much more outstanding than I am—fluent in foreign languages, brilliant at needlework, skilled at winning gold medals and bringing glory to the nation, or at having sons to win their husband's affections. But I couldn't care less about them. The sole objects of my jealousy are those women who happen to be more beautiful than me. Why is that? It's because all those other qualities and talents result from hard work and self-cultivation—it takes a lot of effort to succeed in those aspects—and the difficulty is clear to everyone. But natural beauty is a gift from heaven requiring absolutely no personal effort; whenever I see it, I'm keenly reminded that people can never really be equal in this world.

The escorts at Flowery Immortals were all sitting in a side booth, waiting for guests to choose them. I wanted to make the selection myself, so after I got Chen Xinzhang and the others seated at a table beside the dance floor, I went over to the booth. The lights in the booth were dimmed, and the girls were spread about randomly. When I came in, they appraised me suspiciously, not quite clear what I was up to. I wasn't sure how to get the ball rolling either. But as it happened, a bespectacled man abruptly stumbled in, looking nervous—obviously a beginner—and seeing as I was the only one standing up, asked me: "How about coming over to table fifteen and sitting with us for a while?" All the girls twittered with laughter, and if I hadn't been on work duty, I'd have had a good mind to hire a Hainan tough to smack him around a bit. But it was pretty obvious he had no idea what he was doing, and the lights were too dim to see very much.

In fact, having someone even more clueless around helped to calm me down, and seeing him holding a cigarette, I gave him a friendly suggestion: "Why don't you offer these girls a smoke?"

He had enough sense to grasp what I was saying, and immediately started offering his cigarettes around. As he crouched down to give each girl a light, the glow from his lighter illuminated their pretty faces one by one. Realizing they'd been tricked into revealing themselves, some of them laughed and others swore, and the atmosphere grew much livelier. I was standing behind the man, sizing up the girls myself and feeling extremely worried. What type of girl would those men like, especially Chen Xinzhang? The more I worried, the harder it was to choose, and it wasn't till the lighter flared up for the last time that I decided to let fate take its course and choose her.

She had introduced herself as Lucy. When I heard this I couldn't help giggling to myself, because back in Beijing one of my work colleagues had given herself the same English name, but she was much older and fatter than this Lucy. In fact she was one of the senior managers, and her main specialty seemed to be arriving late for work and leaving early. I remember one time my boyfriend dropped by the office. Knowing how much I hated her, he was amazed to see me holding "Lucy's" fat arm and treating her with great affection. Up to that point, he had probably heard that women could show two completely different faces to the world, one in public and one in private, but to actually witness it in the flesh was quite another matter. I never found out if that shock was the main reason he later decided to dump me.

It was just the same now. I was acting extremely friendly to Lucy, holding her arm and leading her to the place where Mr. Guan and Chen Xinzhang were sitting.

Mr. Guan was not pleased: "What took you so long?"

I replied: "When I'm choosing a girl for Director Chen, of course I need to cover all the bases." Then I introduced everybody. The bodyguard was gone, so it was just the four of us now: Mr. Guan, myself, Chen Xinzhang, and Lucy.

We exchanged pleasantries for a while. I explained to Lucy, "Mr. Guan is a very talented man. He's the director of the Hainan office of X Corporation." Poker-faced, Mr. Guan remained silent. "And this gentleman is the legendary Oil King. If he didn't supply his oil, all the cars in Haikou would have to convert to natural gas!" Chen Xinzhang had his eyes closed, as if he was drunk, but Lucy started laughing—"So what's up with him?" she asked me.

"Can you hold your wine?" I asked her, peeping over at Chen Xinzhang. Seeing him sitting there apparently lost to the world, I whispered to Lucy: "He's probably drunk."

"Who says I'm drunk?" Chen Xinzhang suddenly opened his eyes wide, and grabbed hold of Lucy's hand: "Linda," he said, "I'm not drunk, but you've changed your outfit, haven't you? You can't fool me though!"

Looking at Lucy, she didn't seem that different from most of the other girls waiting in the booth, with their thick exaggerated makeup. Maybe she was prettier than me, or maybe not, but when she was on duty she knew how to make the most of what she had, and she must have given the impression that she was beautiful, otherwise I wouldn't have picked her. I made a special effort to talk to her because Chen Xinzhang was completely bombed and Mr. Guan was acting very reserved, and I didn't want her to feel left out. I must have seemed really friendly, but actually I was feeling so grateful—grateful that in Haikou there was such a profession as this. It was so easy for me to escape my awkward predicament and avoid any ethical dilemmas by politely passing the problem over to someone else and hiding behind her.

Out of this situation I had discovered a new kind of psychological insight: maybe being beautiful was not such a great thing. True, Lucy was beautiful, but she was now being shoved into the fiery pit by me. I should tell every single woman: don't get so worked up if you're not a beauty queen.

Pretty women are not superior to us, they just come before us. They are the ones out on the front lines. They give the rest of us a chance to maintain our purity, because we don't have to deal with all those tricky temptations.

I sat there resting my chin on my hands, feeling a sense of release as I watched the couples on the dance floor. Chen Xinzhang had led Lucy off for a dance, which gave me a chance to get a good look at him. He was actually a good deal shorter than Lucy. As they revolved around, I made sure to look away when Chen Xinzhang was facing me, but when Lucy turned toward me I nodded to her, giving an appreciative smile. I sat there immersed in the scene for a while, but then I suddenly realized I shouldn't be neglecting Mr. Guan, so I jerked my head around to look at him.

He was smoking a cigarette, and when he saw me looking over, he asked: "Why didn't you choose a girl for me?"

I replied: "I'm saving you money! You can satisfy your needs from among your company's staff, can't you?"

In the month or so since I had joined the company, I had done everything by the book, but I had the impression that tonight I had somehow offended him, so I had to do my best to smooth things over with my charm. I believed the words of that old proverb, people won't kick you when you're smiling.

He responded: "In that case, let's dance."

Feeling a bit more relaxed, I walked with him onto the dance floor. We danced the two-step, moving our feet back and forth in the darkness, somehow managing not to tread on each other's toes. He didn't say anything for quite a while. I imagined what he would say when he opened his mouth. Probably it would be: "Why is your mind only focused on saving money and not on making more money?"

Yes, that's what he would say, and I would respond by making an abject apology. As I moved my feet to the music, I tried to think of the best way to give him a good impression. But after a bit more dancing, he declared: "Linda, you think you're really smart, don't you?"

I wasn't expecting this, but I managed to answer with a smile: "Only a little bit smart."

"What do you expect to get from doing this?"

"At least I won't be losing anything from it."

I gave him a challenging look, as if daring him to stay on this topic. I was a master at this kind of suggestive but meaningless patter, and I could go on spouting these verbal paradoxes till the cows came home.

But he decided to change the topic. He sighed and said, "If this deal comes off, I'll give you ten percent; then the two of us won't have to work for a while. That would make you happy, wouldn't it?"

Just then someone bumped into my back, and looking round I saw it was Chen Xinzhang. He was hanging on tight to Lucy's waist, but he still couldn't manage to avoid swaying from side to side. I was about to say hi to Lucy when the beat suddenly quickened and Lucy expertly guided Chen Xinzhang around to the other side of the dance floor.

We kept on doing our moves where we were. I said to Mr. Guan, "Did you see that? If Lucy makes him happy, who's to say your deal won't come off, and then you won't even have to give me ten percent!"

He laughed coldly: "Chen Xinzhang is no fool. He could easily spend his own money to get a girl like Lucy. You think she's worth five hundred thousand?"

I returned the favor with an even colder laugh: "Oh ho, so you think *I'm* worth five hundred thousand? If I was Miss

Asia, do you think I'd have to come all the way down to Hainan to make a living? I'd have made my name in Beijing long ago!"

Probably because I was talking pretty loud, a couple beside us turned to look curiously in our direction. I wasn't sure if it was my loud voice or my sudden burst of moodiness, but Mr. Guan was obviously startled and immediately drew me in closer to his body, as if I was a large loudspeaker that he could somehow muffle by standing in front of me.

Having thus gained an inch, I tried to gain more ground by taking his hand and asking in a much softer tone: "Take a good look at me: do you really think I can bring in five hundred thousand worth of business for you? You'd better stop dreaming, sir."

He did actually gaze at me, and I gazed back at him. We stayed like this for a while, and I sensed that he wasn't really looking to answer my question but just blindly following my lead. Still, he didn't loosen his firm grip on my hand till the music stopped.

When Lucy and Chen Xinzhang came back to sit down, they looked like a pair of lovebirds. Chen Xinzhang was leaning over to Lucy's ear and whispering something, and Lucy was laughing softly while she nibbled on pieces of candy. I hardly saw Lucy say one word—her mouth seemed to have only two functions: laughing and eating snacks.

I whispered to Mr. Guan: "Being an escort looks pretty easy, doesn't it?"

He gave me a sidelong glance: "Why don't you try it for a bit. I'd be surprised if you didn't starve to death!"

I knew Mr. Guan was still preoccupied with that business deal, so I teased him, saying, "I know what Chen Xinzhang is saying to Lucy." But at that moment the music started up again, much louder than before. It was disco now, and the strobe lights were swirling around. We could hardly even see Chen Xinzhang's mouth, let alone hear what he was saying.

In any case, I was sure Chen Xinzhang wasn't interested in the two of us anymore.

Mr. Guan led me outside for a stroll. There was a large garden outside the nightclub planted with artfully arranged tropical flowers. To avoid bumping into people we knew, who might get the wrong idea that we were lovers, we headed for the unlit part of the garden and found a stone bench to sit on.

Mr. Guan asked: "So tell me: what was Chen Xinzhang saying to Lucy?"

"Come back to Beijing with me, you can work in my company and be my second in command!"

Mr. Guan gave me a look that clearly stated this was not what he wanted to hear.

I continued: "You'd better get back inside quick: you don't want to miss some major business deal."

Mr. Guan sighed: "You're not still going on about major deals, are you? It's over."

Hearing him say this, I felt he was being a bit unfair, as if I really was somehow to blame. So I frowned and asked, "Do you really think I could be worth five hundred thousand?" I wanted to get the facts straight and make sure he wasn't getting all worked up for the wrong reasons. True, it was humiliating to think that Mr. Guan would sacrifice me for the sake of five hundred thousand, but if he thought that by sacrificing me he really could get five hundred thousand, he was just being an idiot. Since it was clear the deal wasn't on anymore, I wanted to at least get this fact crystal clear in his mind.

But it turned out Mr. Guan wasn't an idiot after all. With a cold laugh, he replied: "To people like Chen Xinzhang, money is not the point. He just gets a kind of psychological thrill out of proving money can buy him anything he wants."

I said: "Okay, now I get it. I thought you were sacrificing me, but in actual fact it was you putting your head on the block. It's just that I didn't let you offer yourself up as a martyr. That's because even though I want to make money too, I can't do it by humiliating myself."

That's when Mr. Guan began to reproach me: "The thing I really can't stand about you Beijing girls is that most of the time you're always trying to make a bit here and a bit there, but when it comes to doing a really big deal you suddenly get cold feet. I've never seen you showing much consideration for other people before. But now, when we get a real chance, here you start spouting all this morality crap!"

It was true. I knew I'd lost the argument, and didn't even try to defend myself. A frond of some kind of southern palm blew gently against my cheek and I plucked the end of it and fiddled with it, saying, "Of course I came to Hainan because I thought I could become a new person here. There's something about Beijing that stopped me from daring to do things and reaching my full potential. But you shouldn't give up on me yet; who's to say I can't change and learn to be more like Lucy."

He probably thought I was just talking pointless nonsense again, because he didn't respond. But even if some of it was nonsense, surely he could see it contained a bit of sincere feeling too?

We were silent for a while. I thought, *This guy must be pretty dense. Unless I say something really ground shaking, he doesn't seem to have any reaction at all.* I looked him straight in the eye and unleashed the full force of my sincerity: "I know you've been crazily trying to get rich down here. And of course, that's what I want too. But I'll let you in on a true saying."

As expected, he took the bait. "What's that?"

"Actually it's hard to be really depraved."

He sank back into his silence again, but I knew my words had struck a chord this time. He certainly had his unscrupulous side, but he hadn't totally lost his moral compass. For a truly immoral person, there were moneymaking opportunities springing up all over the place! But he was more like someone who tried to make money without sacrificing his soul. Still, he didn't seem to mind me sacrificing my morals for his sake. As for me, I was happy to escape my own predicament by expecting Lucy to sacrifice her morals. It was like toppling dominoes: each one knocked the next until finally the last one made the ultimate sacrifice.

This made me feel a bit guilty again about Lucy. The guilt weighed down on my head like a heavy burden. But I wasn't someone who easily admitted my mistakes, even when I was arguing with my own conscience. I started justifying myself: *I haven't forced her to do anything; whatever she did was of her own free will. And don't forget, this is her job, so if I introduce her to a client, I'm actually helping her, aren't I? Do you expect me to let her starve to death?* Put like this, I sounded like some kind of humanitarian. But whatever the rights or wrongs of the situation, I couldn't deny that everything I had done was to protect myself. No matter how I tried to dress it up, my encounter with Lucy had its roots in my own selfishness.

Snapping out of my thoughts about Lucy, I remembered that I was still sitting beside Mr. Guan. I reached over and shook his shoulder, pleading: "Tell me the truth, won't you? Do we still have a chance with today's business deal?"

Like someone waking from a dream, he stubbed out his cigarette and replied, "No chance."

"Why not?"

"Do you really think Chen Xinzhang is drunk? He's just pretending to save himself some embarrassment."

Finally it hit me like a brick: none of these people are idiots; it's only me who thinks she's Miss Smartypants. I couldn't help blushing a little. Luckily it was a dark night, so no one could see my embarrassment. And I've always been good at consoling myself. Soon I was thinking: I may not be that smart, but at least I didn't do anything really stupid. Only someone like Lucy would willingly go and do stupid things like that. My short-lived sympathy for Lucy disappeared as I once more celebrated having used her to avoid an awkward predicament.

Apparently Mr. Guan divined my thoughts, as he suddenly blurted out: "That Chen Xinzhang is pretty pathetic tonight, no? Even Lucy didn't think much of him."

I was shocked: "What do you mean?"

Mr. Guan looked smug as he started to teach me about Hainan again: "That's something you wouldn't understand. The prime targets for escorts here are people like me who live in Hainan permanently. If they play their cards right with a guy like me, they might get a permanent meal ticket. They're not interested in wasting time on big shots from Beijing who have to rush back home after one night of smoldering passion. What can they hope to get out of that?"

I glanced at Mr. Guan, and realized he was just like me: his self-confidence was built on comparing himself to other people. But I couldn't let him sit there looking so smug, so

I put on my best worried-that-the-sky-might-fall look and asked: "But if people like you never make any money, how can the girls expect to survive? Those one-off clients might not be ideal, but at least it keeps them from being forced out on the street."

Mr. Guan glared at me again, he was clearly fed up with me intentionally playing the wayward child, but for some reason, the more deeply I realized we were actually very similar, the more I wanted to rile him up. In a funny way, it was like I was unflinchingly dissecting myself.

He still hadn't told me what I wanted to hear, so I shook his shoulder again and wheedled him: "Come on: tell me how you knew?"

He knew he had to answer just to shut me up: "Didn't you see how Lucy was constantly eating candy?"

"What's so special about that?"

"She didn't want Chen Xinzhang to kiss her, silly!" He tapped me on the temple like a teacher trying to get a message across to a real retard. I couldn't help bursting out laughing. As I bent over laughing, I thought, *Finally he's got his self-confidence back.* When I'd recovered from my giggling fit, I looked at him again, sizing up his mood. He said slowly: "Was it really that hilarious?"

This time I couldn't think of a clever response, so I stopped laughing.

I'm not sure how long we sat there in the garden, but finally Mr. Guan started wondering what was going on inside and he went back into the nightclub. I was happy to stay outside daydreaming for a bit longer, so I remained sitting on the bench. It was really quite dark. Mr. Guan immediately disappeared into the darkness, and as he walked off, I sensed a kind of bleakness in the silence. On the other hand, maybe it was just the cold air of the deep night seeping into my mind.

At night in the south, the moon hangs low in the sky and the dark leaves of tropical trees are motionless in the pale blue moonlight as if growing out of nothingness. But within that boundless peace is an impulsiveness that startles peoples' hearts. Just a bit earlier I was shoulder to shoulder with everyone else in the dance club, but now it felt like I had discovered a hidden wilderness, completely cut off from the world around me. I tried peering through the surrounding leaves toward the buildings I had just left and saw that they were indeed still brightly glowing, just like before. A couple of women dressed to the nines in glittering outfits walked toward the dance hall. They seemed to be floating on air, but doubtless they were dragging the ball and chain of a mundane existence behind them. This scene helped to calm me down a bit and get a better grip on reality.

A phrase kept bobbing up in my consciousness: people live in a floating world. A floating world . . . tonight this phrase had taken on a whole new meaning. You sink and I float; he floats and she sinks—everything is relative to everything else. These days, when there are no longer any absolute truths, the only way we can carry on living, being proud of ourselves, finding happiness, is by contrasting ourselves with other people. Among those who came here tonight—apart from Lucy who was still a mystery to me—the rest of us were all like that.

Mr. Guan later told me that after he went back in, they opened yet another bottle of liquor. He said every time he had gone out drinking with Chen Xinzhang, he was always the first one to throw in the towel, but that night he was feeling good about himself, so for once he was going to wipe the floor with Chen.

But I didn't know all this when I went back into the club. I just felt relaxed and no longer responsible for anything that happened that night. I was able to look at the scene with a new pair of eyes. And who did I see first but Lucy walking toward the exit.

Immediately I had an impulse to scare her. I abruptly moved into her line of vision and asked in a stentorian tone: "Where do you think you're going?"

Naturally she almost jumped out of her skin, but then seeing it was me, she smiled and replied: "Just going to the ladies room."

"The ladies room?" With my hands behind my back, I appraised her skeptically, putting on my best I-suspect-everyone-and-everything look.

"Did you want something?" Lucy was looking at me cautiously, though I guessed it was feigned caution, as I could see her natural tendency was to be direct and straightforward. I decided I didn't want to play games with her anymore, so I just got straight to the point: "Lucy, tell me truthfully: do you want to go back with Mr. Chen tonight?"

Lucy didn't reply, but just smiled and rolled her eyes. Somehow she had made me look like a naïve fool. Feeling a bit diffident, I tried to explain myself: "I know every job has its own rules, and naturally I don't understand the rules of your line of work, so I hope you're not offended by my bluntness. But I hope you get what I was trying to ask, don't you?"

Still smiling, with an expression like a mother humoring a child, she took my hand and slipped a small packet into my palm.

"What's this?"

"A slice of ginger."

"Is that what you've been eating all this time?"

"Yep."

"What does it taste like?"

"Try it yourself," she replied, then turned and walked away.

I stood rooted to the spot for quite a while, holding the packet of ginger slices, wondering what it all meant.

But one thing I did realize was: I was wrong to think I could escape responsibility for everything that happened that night.

When I finally got back to the table, I was surprised to see Mr. Guan already quite soused. By contrast, Chen Xinzhang was full of beans again. He got up to greet me: "Linda, where did you go? Did your boss send you on an errand?" I replied: "Look at you: memory like a sieve! I was dancing with you all evening. Have you forgotten? Or are you just drunk?"

"You were dancing with me all along?"

Just then Lucy came back, and pointing at her I said: "When I was dancing with you, I was wearing that black dress." My tone was absolutely certain, leaving no room for any doubt whatsoever. Chen Xinzhang looked at Lucy and then back at me: "So it seems there are two Lindas: a dancing Linda and a drinking Linda!" He then lurched toward Lucy, declaring: "You must be Drinking Linda!" Lucy nodded her head. He then pointed at me: "That means you haven't drunk anything yet: let's go somewhere and drink wine together!"

He banged on the table and shouted: "Get me the check!"

Even before the words were out of his mouth, I stood up abruptly to block any waitresses from seeing him. I was not about to let him pay the check again. But after I started heading for the front desk to pay, I realized I didn't have any money. I had to turn back and shake Mr. Guan's shoulder: "Hey, hey: wake up!"

Mr. Guan opened his two bleary eyes: "What's up?" he murmured.

"Go pay the bill."

"What bill?" He still wasn't fully awake.

As bad luck would have it, Chen Xinzhang's bodyguard re-emerged. Chen Xinzhang told him to settle the bill, and I could only watch helplessly as he sauntered off to the front desk. I heard Chen Xinzhang's voice behind me: "Linda: we haven't settled our account yet, have we?"

So off we went to carry on drinking somewhere else.

As our car cruised the streets of Haikou and we looked for a place to drink, I couldn't help feeling I'd already had it up to here with all these tricks. I realized the truth of Mr. Guan's words: all Chen Xinzhang wanted was the feeling of crushing everyone and everything in his path. But his so-called targets really weren't worth crushing. Mr. Guan? All he wanted was money, so what kind of feeling can he give you? And me? I didn't have any money, so I didn't care about losing it. In this situation, I didn't know how the evening would end. I just felt miserable, completely resigned to accepting wherever the driver decided to take us.

But actually things weren't as bad as I thought. Chen Xinzhang was already pretty drunk by now: he just wanted to make sure that either I or Mr. Guan was more drunk than he was. He cared more about liquor than sex: that's what I found out during that night of crazy drinking.

We found a cozy little wine bar, and I asked: "What are you drinking?"

"Gotta have the hard stuff!" Surprisingly it was Mr. Guan, who had slept all the way and had now suddenly sprung back to life. I wasn't sure how this happened: it seemed there was no clear line between being drunk and sober. It was all a matter of will power. Just as Mr. Guan earlier suspected Chen Xinzhang wasn't really drunk at all, I now suspected Mr. Guan. In any case, now that he was awake, the atmosphere grew much more lively. Even Lucy perked up a bit, despite Chen Xinzhang constantly repeating that she was Drinking Linda who wasn't allowed to have any more wine tonight.

"Dancing Linda," Chen Xinzhang got up and staggered toward me holding a glass: "Finish this one off!"

"Finish it!" Mr. Guan chimed in. I thought he was just sitting on the sidelines, but he too had finished off a glass.

"Excellent!" Lucy exclaimed, and refilled Mr. Guan's glass.

Everyone seemed to have unlimited capacity, gulping down one glass after another, nobody willing to admit defeat. But inside I knew I was losing control. It was the first time in my life that I'd truly been totally drunk. Looking back on that night, I can still feel exactly what it was like. It was as if everything around me was getting in my way. Whenever I tried to move forward, a massive force seemed to block me; but when I tried to stand still, another massive force suddenly unblocked me and pushed me from behind until I fell over.

Just when I was struggling with these contradictory forces, Chen Xinzhang came toward me with yet another glass: "Linda, finish this one off!"

With a huge effort, I controlled myself, and in a slurring voice replied: "Why do you keep on repeating the same sentence? Don't you have anything else to say?"

"The words may change but the wine remains the same: you still have to drink up."

I shot back: "Who says I have to drink it? I don't even

know who you are!"

"Those who drink wine with friends think nothing of emptying a thousand cups. If you can finish off this last glass, I promise to supply your boss with five hundred thousand worth of oil."

I could feel my palms sweating. If this was true, it really wasn't that hard, and it would certainly stop Mr. Guan from laying the blame on me. But even if it was easy enough in itself, I still felt I was being forced into it. Had I wasted the whole evening worrying about losing my principles only to let Chen Xinzhang get the better of me in the end?

I strongly sensed that I was already on the verge of defeat. I needed something to grab hold of, like a table or a chair, to keep from falling over. But when I clenched my fist, I felt something soft and sticky in my palm. It was the packet of ginger slices. The cheap packaging had already been soaked ragged by my sweaty hands, and I could feel the irregular shapes and patterned texture of the candy inside. Looking up, I saw Lucy sitting opposite. In the dim lights, her face was hidden, but the black outline of her mascara and her crimson red lipstick seemed to pulse back and forth in the smoke-filled atmosphere.

Just when I least expected it, Mr. Guan stood up and held out his glass to Chen Xinzhang: "I really appreciate Director Chen's generous offer," he said. "But to tell the truth, I really couldn't scrape together the financing to buy five hundred thousand barrels of oil. So let's not give Linda any more trouble. I'll finish this one off, and then let's just be friends, okay?"

All of a sudden I felt totally exhausted, and tears started flowing down my face. Trying to hide my distress, I struggled to my feet and staggered off to the bathroom.

The next day I called Lucy and found out what happened after I left.

She said Mr. Guan and Chen Xinzhang found some much bigger glasses and filled them to the brim. Mr. Guan emptied his glass first, and all the onlookers shouted their approval and gave him a big round of applause. Then it was Chen Xinzhang's turn. He couldn't exactly refuse, not with everyone looking on, so he finished his glass in one shot. There was another big round of applause. But then Chen Xinzhang noisily smacked his lips and with enormous satisfaction declared: "That lemonade tasted great!"

Mr. Guan, having been made to look like a buffoon, felt pretty miffed about this. But to me it made a lot of sense: it was like the perfect end to the story. Ultimately Chen Xinzhang still managed to eke out his little victory, or at least that's what he would have thought. Of course maybe it was just his way of saving face, and possibly those glasses did actually contain the infamous Erguotou liquor. If so, he must have really felt it burning in his throat!

Lucy laughed as she told me: "You really shouldn't try getting into any contests with a man like Chen Xinzhang!" She also said: "That Mr. Guan knows how to behave, though. Seems there are still some people left in the world who have sincere feelings . . ." I understood what Lucy was trying to say, though I thought it was going a bit far to call them "sincere feelings." I couldn't accept that interpretation. But I put it down to her lack of education.

Subsequently, while I was still staying in Hainan, Lucy would often call me, even though I seldom called her. Possibly she thought this memorable mission had made us comrades-in-arms. I didn't want to encourage that notion. But I did sometimes go to the store she recommended to buy ginger slices. In a hot and humid place like Hainan, not many people ate snacks like that, so it was hard to find a place that sold them.

BEIJING WOMAN

X U XINGLI, ONE OF THE WAITRESSES IN THE FAST FOOD diner, said to her boss, Lin Baihui: "My sister's come down."

For a moment, Lin Baihui didn't get what she was talking about—"Come down? Where from?"

Xu Xingli replied, "From our village, of course."

Lin Baihui then realized that Xu Xingli's village was up around Zhangjiakou, so when people from there talked about Beijing they probably visualized a map with Beijing to the lower right. That's why she said "come down." Now that she came to think of it, Lin Baihui did recall Xu Xingli prattling on about her younger sister "planning to come down," but with so many other things to worry about she had put it out of her mind.

The staff in the diner came from all over the place. Every dialect you can imagine was represented there. One waitress from the Northeast had just started her first day working in the diner when a customer asked her for some vinegar. She replied: "Weet a mawment, sir, I'll seek some foor ya." Her tones were all over the place too.

Running a diner involved lots of little frustrations, which often put Lin Baihui in a bad mood. She did have some self-control. She knew it was wrong to lose her temper with the

111

staff for no reason. So her criticism of their non-standard regional dialects acted as the main outlet for her suppressed irritation. As soon as she felt fed up, she would frown at them and tell them they couldn't say this and couldn't say that, just like a bitter old spinster blaming everyone else for her own troubles. Lin Baihui was only in her early thirties, but she had been a teacher before, and this was surely the source of her ingrained tendency to promote standard Chinese over regionalisms. It was also the source of her hypocrisy.

Of course, the staff saw right through her. They knew she was just lashing out at them because of her own emotional hang-ups, and she couldn't fire them just for speaking a different dialect. They not only failed to correct their speaking habits but sometimes even forcefully challenged her logic. For instance, Lin Baihui felt pained when they used phrases like "totally cool!" and "O.M.G.!" but they argued with some conviction that these were not dialect words: they had never heard anyone in their home villages talk like that: "We learned them after we came to Beijing, so they must be Beijing Chinese!" they would declare, giving her an impudent look that implied: You call yourself a Beijing woman? You don't even understand your own language!

When she was clearheaded, Lin Baihui would simply denounce these assertions and strongly deny that such phrases were Beijing Chinese. But sometimes her staff would manage to tempt her into arguing back. She would declare: "So what if it's Beijing Chinese? You should speak Standard Chinese, not Beijing Chinese!" Her staff would then think she was completely off her rocker, full of self-contradictions, trying to make them believe that Beijing Chinese and Standard Chinese were different. "So who are we s'posed to learn Standard Chinese from? If we can't learn from Beijing people, where are we s'posed to find this phantom 'Standard Chinese' speaker?" In this way, Lin Baihui lost her authority, at least in matters of linguistics.

This was the general context for Xu Xingli and Lin Baihui's conversation. It was around ten o'clock in the morning, and Lin Baihui had just arrived at the diner, and Lin Baihui had mainly been moaning about the problems she had encountered during her early morning errands.

She had gotten up really early that morning to deal with some red tape at the Small Business Bureau. The Bureau was in a small, winding back street in the Guandongdian district. It was impossible to find a parking space there, so Lin Baihui had to park in the lot under the Blue Island Building, then cross the main road to Guandongdian. After she crossed the road, she walked through a patch of greenery where several people were milling about, hands in their pockets, scanning the passersby on the street. As soon as they saw Lin Baihui, they came over and whispered: "Wanna buy a degree? Whatever you need, we've got it: university, college, tech school, entrance exam certificates, you name it." Seeing these guys trying to make a living like this, Lin Baihui was amused and thought: *Why should I buy a degree from you? I already graduated from a top university.* But when she came out of the Bureau and walked past again, they still pestered her with their surreptitious whispers: "Wanna buy a degree?" This time she got a bit fed up. *Since when did I become a target for fake college degree sellers?* she wondered. "Do I really look like the kind of loser who needs a fake degree to cheat her way into a job?" She quickly put on her glasses to check that the pedestrian light was green and escaped from them, crossing the main road. When she got back to the parking lot, she suddenly realized: *They must have seen how dejected and crestfallen I was after banging my head against the brick wall of the Small Business Bureau!*

Lin Baihui was still in that mood when she heard Xu announce that her younger sister had "come down." Once she understood what Xu Xingli was going on about, it was the perfect excuse for her to release some of her tension onto Xu by grimacing and barking: "You should speak Standard Chinese!" Xu Xingli looked embarrassed and replied: "Ms. Lin, I find it so difficult to learn Beijing Chinese."

But her self-criticism touched a raw nerve with Lin Baihui: she really couldn't abide this mindless confusion of Beijing Chinese with Standard Chinese. She re-emphasized the point for the umpteenth time: "I'm asking you to learn Standard Chinese, not Beijing Chinese. I'm not engaging in some kind of 'war of the dialects' here!" Lin Baihui belonged to the generation that had been students when the winds of democracy had blown through the education system, but she hadn't quite taken in the whole picture. As a result, even though she didn't behave democratically, if someone told her she was not being democratic, she would blush and feel slightly guilty about it.

So she tried to hide her irritation and explain the point more gently. Xu Xingli didn't bother to defend herself. Maybe she thought it was a waste of time. Instead she asked pragmatically: "So how am I supposed to say it then?" Lin Baihui gave her a textbook reply: "My sister has arrived in Beijing."

"But she hasn't arrived: she won't arrive till the day after tomorrow!"

"Well in that case you should say: my sister will arrive in Beijing the day after tomorrow."

"Okay, my sister will arrive in Beijing the day after tomorrow," Xu Xingli parroted, then looked expectantly at Lin Baihui. Lin Baihui thought she was waiting for her approval, so she said: "Good, very good," then turned to walk away.

Xu Xingli immediately called after her: "But Ms. Lin, I had something to ask you!"

Oh yes, Lin Baihui thought, *she must have something on her mind. She wouldn't have come to see me just to get a lesson in Standard Chinese!*

"What did you want to ask?"

Xu Xingli hung her head and fiddled with the edge of her apron, then said haltingly: "I don't know how to say it in Standard Chinese." It was just after ten in the morning, and the breakfast rush was over. The lunchtime crowd had not arrived yet, so it was a good time to talk; but on the other hand, they had already used up several minutes wrangling about linguistic niceties, and the busy lunch hour was fast approaching. Lin Baihui sighed and gave in, "Just say what you have to say. I don't care what dialect you use!"

Xu Xingli then felt free to talk. It turned out her younger sister had suffered a nervous breakdown when she was very young, and even though she had recovered, her family thought she was too vulnerable to leave her home village and look for work. But there wasn't much work available in their village, and as she got older she couldn't endure sitting around at home doing nothing. Two years ago she had announced to her family: next time my big sister comes home for the holidays, I'm going down to Beijing with her. That was the reason why Xu Xingli's parents hadn't allowed her to return home and see her family for the past two Chinese New Year holidays.

Lin Baihui muttered, "No wonder!" This year, Lin Baihui had hesitated whether to keep the diner open over Chinese New Year, but she had been happily surprised when Xu Xingli volunteered to give up her holiday. She had even publicly praised Xu and promised to pay her overtime. Xu Xingli was delighted by this too, and nobly declared that she didn't mind giving up her New Year celebration to help the diner's business flourish. Since it was only ten days after Chinese New Year, her words were still fresh in Lin Baihui's memory.

When she heard Lin Baihui say "no wonder," Xu Xingli probably realized she had let the cat out of the bag, and she felt a bit embarrassed. Her head gave a nervous twitch. But Lin Baihui thought there was no need for her to be embarrassed. *It's perfectly understandable. It's not as if she's really going to sacrifice herself for my sake, and I have no right to force her to do that.* Mind you, Xu Xingli wasn't the only staff member who papered over the truth with fancy words. One young guy from Anhui was a keen worker with deft hands. Lin Baihui really liked him, and wanted to train him to do skilled jobs like making pancakes. She once asked him, "Do you want to get ahead here? How about I let you learn some cooking skills in the kitchen?" Lin Baihui was only expecting him to say thanks, but she was completely shocked when this young guy declared with a straight face: "I'll do anything you ask. I want to dedicate my whole being one hundred and ten percent to this diner!"

Now seeing Xu Xingli squirming with embarrassment, Lin Baihui felt like teasing her. "If that's the real reason you didn't go home, why didn't you say so last week?" But surprisingly Xu Xingli took it seriously, and with a convincing sob tried to justify herself: "But I thought you wanted us to speak Beijing Chinese?"

Lin Baihui thought to herself: *She must be kidding! Surely it's possible to dress up the truth with fancy words in her local dialect too. On the other hand, if she really used her local dialect, I certainly wouldn't have any idea what she was talking about.* Instead of belaboring the point, she focused on the current situation. Why was Xu Xingli mentioning her younger sister? Lin Baihui noticed that even though Xu Xingli was looking down, she kept glancing up to see Lin Baihui's reaction. This was the first time Lin Baihui had closely observed Xu Xingli and noticed how unusual she looked. Her two large, protruding cheeks were set very high on her face, and her eyes were just thin slits, as if squeezed together between her high cheeks and her forehead. Lin Baihui had never actually noticed her eyes before: she had always just looked at her cheekbones and then looked away. Probably it was because her eyes were not that easy to see, and Lin Baihui couldn't be bothered to make the extra effort. But today she suddenly discovered how contradictory Xu Xingli looked— when you only saw her plump cheeks, you would get the impression that she was a bit slow; but when you noticed her narrow eyes, you would get a different impression, that she was actually quite sharp-witted. In some ways, she was no different from many of the other service staff: you could never really tell if they were smart or foolish. It was just that in Xu Xingli's case, the ambiguity was directly and classically inscribed on her face.

Lin Baihui's curiosity got the better of her. She asked: "Since you didn't go back home this time, how can your sister come down here by herself?"

Xu Xingli replied: "Yeah well, if Dad was still back home, he would've stopped her coming, but since he came down to Beijing, she's not gonna listen to anyone else. No one's gonna get in her way now."

"So where's your dad working then?"

"Pretty close by—he's a street sweeper around here."

"How come your whole family lives around here now?"

Xu Xingli laughed. "It's not just my family, the whole village lives around here now!" She then asked Lin Baihui: "Ms. Lin, could you let Erli come and work in the diner?"

Xu Xingli had obviously been working up to this. Lin Baihui thought for a moment then told her it wasn't right to have relatives working in the same diner. Xu Xingli persisted: "But she could work in the other location, couldn't she?"

There was a vacancy at Lin's other diner, but could she really do the job? Xu Xingli insisted that she could. "She wouldn't have any problem, she can work hard without any complaints. The only thing she can't stand is people bullying her—that always makes her ill." Hearing this, Lin Baihui burst out laughing. She thought of all the grief she had to put up with at the Small Business Bureau, and really wished she could catch a disease like that, to be able to go sick in the head at the first sign of bullying, to lash out at people and curse them without being held responsible for it. She laughed hysterically at this thought while Xu Xingli just stared at her with a dumb look on her face. Finally, realizing she was not behaving appropriately, Lin Baihui controlled herself and said with a poker face, "Well if you're going to have a character flaw, that's a good one to have!" She thought she made it clear she was joking, but Xu Xingli seemed to think she was serious.

As Lin Baihui recalled, that was all she and Xu Xingli talked about, and then they had to go and deal with the lunchtime rush hour. She didn't remember giving any promises to Xu Xingli, but somehow Xu Xingli thought she had. As far as she was concerned, Lin Baihui's evaluation of Erli was: there's nothing wrong with her, or if there is anything wrong with her, it's not a problem. Xu Xingli was convinced she had successfully recommended Erli for the job, and that Lin Baihui liked her sister a lot.

That this misunderstanding later caused Lin Baihui lots of trouble was really all her own fault. Even though she had to deal with these working girls every day, she still hadn't learned how to communicate with them properly. They could only comprehend the simplest and most direct instructions. Lin Baihui's subtle wit went right over their heads—it was too "Beijing" for them to handle. All they could do was pick out a few words and phrases that they understood, and try to piece them together into a cruder but simpler message.

The next day was the eleventh day after the Chinese New Year, a day when huge numbers of migrant workers surged back to Beijing from their rural villages. All a diner had to do was post up a "help wanted" notice, and immediately workers would line up to be interviewed. This was the first year that Lin Baihui had operated her diners, so she wasn't familiar with this routine, but her manager had plenty of experience. His name was Ma, and though he was just young lad from Sichuan in his early twenties, he had been managing restaurants for quite a while already. That day he had posted a recruitment notice on the diner window, but before twenty minutes had passed, a supervising officer from the city's urban management bureau rolled up and told him to remove it, otherwise he'd be in big trouble for hiring migrant workers without a permit. When Lin Baihui arrived at the diner, she saw one of the staff scraping the bits of glue off the glass where the notice had been. "How can we find

119

new staff without a help wanted sign?" she asked Ma. "I've interviewed four applicants already, and more'll come soon," Ma replied smugly. That's exactly what happened: Ma called Lin Baihui in the evening to report that he had filled all the vacancies in both her diners. By that time she was already driving home, and after hearing this news she couldn't help feeling a little smug herself. Hiring Ma to manage the diners was the best thing she had done since starting her business. In many respects he was far more experienced than she was. He certainly had the potential to become a restaurant owner himself.

The following day was the warmest since the New Year. The wind had died down too. Driving to work, Lin Baihui kept the car window down for the whole trip, which put her in a great mood. Since January first that year, the Beijing government had mandated much stricter regulations for car exhaust emissions. They were even stricter than in the United States. The media didn't make this comparison, but Lin Baihui liked to make it herself, because she had lived in the U.S. for two years, and the blue skies and white clouds over there had made a deep impression on her. After she came back to China, blue skies and white clouds had pretty much become a thing of the past. Some of her friends who lived in America and occasionally visited Beijing would start complaining about the poor air quality and pollution as soon as they got off the plane. But Lin Baihui saw this as a visitor's psychology: they could complain because they were soon heading back to the U.S. By contrast, Lin Baihui planned to stay in China and develop her career there, so she refused to complain about the pollution even if it made her miserable. The only way to deal with it was to put all memories of

America out of her mind, pretending they didn't exist.

But late last year she read in the paper that Beijing was about to regulate exhaust fumes, and she immediately found herself thinking These emission standards are stricter than those in Los Angeles! Clearly she hadn't quite managed to completely forget those blue skies and white clouds of America.

So this morning, she kept the car windows open all the way, enjoying the unusually clear morning air. But as she came up to the final right turn before reaching the diner, a bus suddenly started off in front of her and belched out a thick black cloud of smoke. For an instant, Lin Baihui had the illusion of being in a deep ocean. She recalled a book she had read when she was very young which described how deep sea squid would spurt out black ink to confuse their predators. But over twenty years had passed since she had read that book, and she couldn't for the life of her remember whether this was a scientific fact or just a fairy tale. Ruing her poor memory, which was obviously a sign of middle age, she yanked the steering wheel to the right, hoping to penetrate the black curtain of smoke. Swerving out she looked ahead but forgot to check behind—until she heard a crunching sound. She had cut off a pedicab and a large iron shovel protruding from the front had hit her rear side window.

The pedicab rider quickly dismounted, and Lin Baihui stopped her car and stuck her head out the window. In no time a crowd of onlookers gathered round to enjoy the spectacle. But actually there was no visible damage to either vehicle. Lin Baihui said "Really sorry about that," and the rider politely replied: "No problem. Have a good day, Boss Lin." Lin Baihui was startled, and some of the onlookers also looked surprised, but the rider explained: "My daughter works in your diner." Lin Baihui noticed that he too had those distinctive high protruding cheekbones and thought to herself, *This must be Xu Xingli's dad.*

Lin Baihui apologized once more, then started her car and continued driving around the corner to the diner. As she approached the diner, she saw someone dressed in bright red standing on the steps outside the front door. When Lin Baihui parked her car in front of the diner, that person bent down to look inside and smiled at her. Lin Baihui decided that only someone just off the train from the countryside would smile like that for no reason, and this impression was reinforced by the girl's clothes. From a distance, she appeared to be wearing a single red outfit, but closer up it was clear that her jacket and pants were two different shades of red. The other distinctive feature of this girl was her high protruding cheekbones, which caused her eyes to disappear completely when she smiled. If this wasn't a member of Xu Xingli's family, it was definitely someone from the same village!

Lin Baihui got out of her car, took out her backpack and locked the door. While she was doing this, several customers had walked up the steps to the diner, and that girl had turned to smile at them and open the door for them. She was standing a bit too far away from the door, but for some reason she didn't think to move closer; instead she bent the top half of her body over and stretched her arm out to reach the door, leaving her legs in the same position. The customers were startled by this, as she clearly wasn't one of the welcoming staff, but she was making a sincere if clumsy effort to help them. After they went in, the guests couldn't help turning to take another look at this strange person.

Lin Baihui thought this must be some crazy lark that Ma had come up with. Generally speaking Ma was a smart guy, but every now and then he would get some idiotic idea into his head about how they could differentiate themselves from the competition. Lin Baihui was quite short-tempered, and inwardly she swore at Ma—what game is he playing at? This is a respectable diner, not some kind of truck-stop escort service! She stomped into the diner and shouted: "Where's the manager?" Ma wasn't around, but Xu Xingli was busy waiting tables, and when she saw Lin Baihui she pointed at the door and said: "Ms. Lin, that's Erli!" Lin Baihui finally understood: "Oh, right, she's come down."

Ma then came running out of the kitchen at the back and asked her what was wrong. Lin Baihui blushed and swallowed the choice swear words she'd been planning to unleash on Ma. Instead she raised a couple of minor issues relating to the business. *don't speak her mind*

Seeing more and more customers coming in, Lin Baihui walked to the front door and tapped Erli on the shoulder. Erli turned and greeted her warmly: "Hello Ms. Lin." Lin Baihui coolly acknowledged the greeting, then said: "You'd better go inside and wait in your sister's dormitory. Don't come out and get in peoples' way." Erli didn't seem to catch her drift, so Lin Baihui re-emphasized the point: "Stop getting in peoples' way, do you understand?" Erli then looked crestfallen and walked inside hanging her head, continuing through to the back where the staff dormitory was located. Some of the customers turned to look at her again, and one of the regular customers laughed and said to Lin Baihui: "Why not just let her stand there: it is March Fifth after all!" March Fifth was when everyone was meant to imitate the Communist martyr Lei Feng by helping out their neighbors. Lin Baihui laughed at this remark, but she didn't reply.

Lin Baihui spent the whole lunch-hour rush in the kitchen

at the back. The order slips kept coming through from the dining room, and when Lin saw them all arranged in a long line on the counter she felt elated. As each order was cooked, the relevant order slip would be removed, and gradually the line of slips diminished until the last order was filled. The chefs wiped the sweat off their faces and Lin Baihui was relieved: *Luckily there's no such thing as an everlasting banquet.*

Lin Baihui walked through to the dining room. It had been completely packed earlier but now it was empty, except for one couple in the far corner who lingered awhile, chatting over their leftover stew and rice. A warm feeling welled up in Lin Baihui's heart when she saw these lovebirds, but then when she thought about it, she realized this was the wrong attitude to take. The customers she should appreciate were those who surged in like a tide then, after wolfing down their lunch, equally quickly surged out again. They were the ones who came here to eat, unlike this couple who were obviously here just to take up space and chat.

As the owner of the diner, Lin Baihui quite often caught herself taking the wrong attitude like this, and when it happened she would scold herself: "You still don't know how to play your role properly!" But how should a real boss behave? She didn't know where she should even look to find a proper role model.

Just then Xu Xingli padded over to her and called out: "Ms. Lin!" This reminded Lin Baihui that she still had to deal with Xu Xingli's sister. She was about to tell her not to let her sister stand outside the doorway, but Xu Xingli jumped in first: "When are you going to send Erli over to the other location?"

Lin Baihui didn't seem to notice the assumption in Xu

Xingli's question—that Erli had already been hired and the only thing left was to fix the starting date. "We've filled all the positions at the other location now—Manager Ma finished recruiting last week." Xu Xingli's expression suddenly turned fierce. Lin Baihui noticed her dissatisfaction, but she stuck to her guns: what kind of boss would she be if she let her staff push her around like that?

Xu Xingli was clearly fed up, but instead of complaining she just stood there in stubborn silence, avoiding eye contact. Lin Baihui wanted to give her a good telling off, but she didn't know where to start, so instead she tried persuasion. "There're jobs available all over the place right now, she could try the neighbor's place for a start." The neighbor's place was also a restaurant. Xu Xingli sniffed, treating Lin Baihui's suggestion with complete indifference. She distinctly remembered that Lin Baihui had agreed she would not reject Erli. After she had translated Lin Baihui's Beijing-style remark into a language she could understand, it had become "That kind of defect is one that can easily be overcome." But listening to her now, it was clear she had changed her mind and was trying to foist Erli off on someone else. Xu Xingli thought to herself, *You call yourself a boss, but you can't even stick to what you said.* It was just like the time Lin Baihui had first told them all to speak Beijing Chinese, but then turned round and said even Beijing Chinese wasn't right! As she recalled Lin Baihui's longstanding failure to stick to what she said, Xu Xingli's heart filled with resentment.

Lin Baihui persisted. "It's really easy to find work right now. Look at our diner, last week we hired five people all at once. I'm sure most other restaurants are like that too." Xu Xingli didn't seem to be paying attention. She seemed to be daydreaming: "There's not much we can do now anyway—

she's asleep," she said.

"I guess she's tired after taking that long train ride," Lin Baihui replied.

Xu Xingli re-focused her attention, "She's a bit tired, but if you ask her to start working now, she won't have any problem." Lin Baihui then recalled the strange image of Erli opening the door for the customers: she certainly didn't look even a bit tired when she was doing that.

After Xu Xingli finished her shift, she went back to the dormitory. Lin Baihui was about to go home, but then she remembered a couple of things she had to tell Ma. Since Ma was out buying supplies, she decided to sit for a while and read the newspaper in one of the chairs by the window. Although she was the boss now, she still hadn't changed some of the habits she used to have as a state employee, and one of these was having a regular tea break to read the newspaper.

She didn't have any particular reason for reading the paper, she just enjoyed browsing through the columns. When the world was transformed into words it became so much simpler and clearer. In this sense, Lin Baihui was similar to the staff in her diner. Just like them, she liked to reinterpret complex and unfamiliar things so they became simple and understandable.

Whatever the reason, it made her feel happy to pass the time reading. As she sat there, the early spring sky kept changing: one moment it was crystal clear; the next moment a bunch of large clouds came floating over. As they passed the window, their shadows fell onto Lin Baihui's newspaper. Lin Baihui was so engrossed in her reading that she didn't notice the sun disappearing at all, except that it meant she no longer had to squint to see the words, and the reading became even more enjoyable.

But suddenly she had a feeling that someone was watching her. Looking up from the paper, she saw Erli come creeping out from the direction of the dormitory. As Erli emerged, she kept her eyes on Lin Baihui's every move, like a small animal warily observing a dangerous predator. Lin Baihui found this funny. *Erli clearly doesn't realize that the last thing I want to do is catch her: she's completely free to go!* She pretended to be absorbed in the newspaper while looking at Erli out of the corner of her eye. She discovered that Erli was walking in a very strange manner: her upper body remained stiff, but she would stretch out each leg before moving forward as if testing the surface, all the time keeping her eyes fixed on Lin Baihui. Lin Baihui had seen many variety shows on television, and when the performers wanted to portray a country bumpkin they would use the same kind of body language. Lin Baihui had always assumed it was just a stereotype, but apparently it did have some basis in reality! After coming to this conclusion, Lin Baihui buried her face in the newspaper once more.

She read a few more lines, but soon her curiosity got the better of her, and she looked up again. She was startled to find Erli standing right beside her, and Erli looked just as startled to see her shocked reaction. But actually there was a transparent glass panel separating them which Erli had apparently not noticed. Lin Baihui flicked her newspaper against the glass, and Erli finally realized it was there and she laughed. Apparently Lin Baihui the predator was not going to eat her after all.

In the gentle afternoon light, Lin Baihui could see that Erli was prettier than her elder sister. Lin Baihui tried to analyze this vague impression. True, Erli had those distinctive protruding cheekbones, but her cheeks were not as high as Xu Xingli's, so they didn't obscure her eyes; they just made her face seem rounder. It was clear from her appearance that she had had a protected childhood: her face was pale, plump and smooth with a ruddy hue, not tanned and rough from working outside in all kinds of weather. To borrow a stock phrase from martial arts fiction, her skin seemed so soft that one puff of wind could melt it. Lin Baihui thought to herself: *This Erli doesn't look like a good worker.* The same protruding cheekbones on Xu Xingli's face made you feel that she could take all of life's humiliations and bury them or endure them, but on Erli's face you felt that one gentle tap would be sufficient to break them.

Looking at Erli, Lin Baihui laughed. Although she seldom laughed with her staff, she found it much easier to lighten up with people whose interests were not bound up with her own.

Erli responded with another laugh then turned and went out the front door and down the steps outside. Lin Baihui noticed she had tied her hair back with a bright red flower ornament, which added a third shade of red to her outfit. Dressed completely in red with a crimson flower in her hair, this teenager walked down the steps and out to the curbside. Viewed from up close her outfit was pretty ugly, but from a distance, once it became part of the general scenery, it improved greatly. Erli seemed to turn into a bright point of light on the street, constantly drawing Lin Baihui's gaze back to her.

The street side of the diner consisted of four large glass windows, with each glass panel shaped like a widescreen television. Lin Baihui's gaze followed Erli as she walked from one side of the first screen to the other side, then briefly lost sight of her until she reappeared in the next screen, like an extended take in a movie.

As Lin Baihui watched this movie of Erli's progress, she also took in the background street scene. Previously she had never done this: she normally just quickly glanced outside as if to acknowledge the street's presence, but without noticing any details. Today it seemed like Erli was unrolling an animated scroll before her eyes, giving Lin Baihui the time to appreciate every distinct scene in the proper sequence. In the first scene, she saw a brick building reinforced with earthquake-resistant metal hoops, and beside it a high tower. The next scene started with the tower again then moved to a shopping mall. In the third scene she saw lots of pedestrians all heading back toward the second scene, and following them back she saw they all went into the shopping mall. Distracted by the shoppers, she momentarily lost track of Erli, and when she caught up with her again, Erli was already well into the fourth scene, in fact almost out of the picture.

She's probably gone to look for her dad. Hopefully things will go smoothly for her and she'll find a job somewhere else.

The evening rush had now descended on the diner, but in the midst of the rush Xu Xingli found a minute to come over to Lin Baihui and say: "Ms. Lin, I've been too busy to find a job for Erli yet. Is it okay if she stays here for two more days?" Lin Baihui replied: "Don't you know the Rules of the Diner? Non-staff aren't permitted to stay in the dormitories." Xu Xingli said: "I didn't know we had a rule like that." Lin Baihui herself wasn't completely sure if this was one of the Rules of the Diner. She had certainly written out several pages of rules and regulations, but even she couldn't remember them all, so she changed the subject: "I thought your dad was here too?" Xu Xingli replied: "Yes, but he stays in a drafty big old shed with a dozen other workers, and all of them are men, so it's not suitable for Erli to stay there." Lin Baihui reluctantly agreed: "Well okay, just for now."

She went back to her office and looked up the Rules of the Diner, only to find that in fact there was no such rule prohibiting friends and relatives from staying in the dormitory. She couldn't help feeling irritated. She knew it was her own omission, just one of many things she thought she had done but actually hadn't. But since the situation was like this, she couldn't very well insert a new rule and apply it retroactively. That would make her look capricious, using arbitrary rule-making to oppress her staff. She would have to wait until Erli left, then make the revision and never allow any outsiders to stay in the dormitory again.

She wasn't pleased about the Erli situation, but soon put it out of her head. There were too many other things for her to deal with. One day, as she was driving along, her cellphone rang and it was Ma, in a great state of fear and agitation, telling her there was trouble at the diner. Lin Baihui immediately assumed some thugs had come to smash the place up, so she told him: "Call the police quick!" But Ma replied: "It's the police who are causing the trouble!" Lin Baihui thought this was ludicrous: "Why are you scared of the police?" But Ma still didn't calm down: "You'd better come over here anyway, 'cause I can't deal with it."

I sure hope it's not some previous offence Ma committed, and the police have finally caught up with him. She had little choice but to cancel her plans for that day and rush over to the diner. All the way she was trying to plan what she would say to the police. Of course she would start by denying all knowledge of Ma's murky past. This wasn't just deflecting responsibility from herself, it was actually true. As she planned her response, she came to a right turn, and was once again engulfed in smoke from the exhaust of a public bus in front of her. This time she didn't try any sudden maneuvers, but instead reduced her speed to escape the cloud of smoke. She had already slowed down before this, in preparation for the right turn, and now she really felt like she was in a small boat that had lost power in the middle of a powerful river current. From outside it didn't seem that way—observers would have seen the boat moving forward—but the boat's pilot knew very well that she no longer had the ability to go where she wanted to go.

Fortunately this feeling was short lived. The black smoke dispersed without incident, and she was surrounded by clear air once more. She rounded the bend and drove up to the front of the diner. Getting out of the car, nothing seemed to be amiss. The staff were all doing their allotted tasks: cleaning the windows, sweeping the entrance. It was a picture of peaceful tranquillity, with no hint of any reason for Ma's terror. Entering the diner, she saw that indeed a policeman was sitting there conspicuously, drinking tea from a disposable paper cup.

Lin Baihui walked up to him quickly and greeted him, introducing herself as the owner of the diner. She explained she had been running some errands, but hearing that he was here for an inspection she had come back as soon as possible. The policeman was in his early thirties, slightly plump, with a pale, well-scrubbed face. After listening to Lin Baihui's explanation, he took another sip of tea then put down his cup and lit a cigarette. Finally he opened his mouth to speak: "Where are you from?"

Lin Baihui was not sure how to respond to this, but after a moment's thought she replied: "I'm from this diner." After hearing this irrelevant answer, the policeman said nothing at first, but instead retrieved a notebook from his case. He asked: "How many people work in this diner?" Lin Baihui replied: "Eighteen, probably." The policeman declared: "Aren't you the boss? Don't you even know the exact number?" Lin Baihui responded: "I don't come here every day: I leave the day-to-day business to my manager. I can call him out here if you like." The policeman waved off this suggestion, causing bits of ash to fall from his cigarette: "Don't bother: I already talked to your manager."

Hearing him say this, Lin Baihui realized she was getting worked up over nothing, and Ma hadn't committed any crimes. But after the officer wrote the number 18 in his notebook, he continued in a much more severe tone: "Have you got all their temporary residence permits sorted out?" Lin Baihui replied hesitantly: "I'm pretty sure they've all been sorted out." She had definitely reminded Ma to get the staff residence permits approved, but because there were fees to pay, she hadn't made much effort to follow up on it, and under this intense questioning, she couldn't be completely sure if it had been done. She looked around and grabbed the closest waitress, telling her: "Go and ask Manager Ma to come out." The waitress went off to do her bidding.

The police officer didn't seem interested—doubtless he had already asked Ma before Lin Baihui came back—and he wrote in his notebook the words "not yet approved." Then he stood up and said to Lin Baihui: "I won't fine you today, but I'll be back again next week for another inspection, and if you can't produce all the necessary permits, I'll have to penalize you by the book." Lin Baihui nodded incessantly—"I appreciate that," she said. When incidents like this happened, she was always slow to react. She still hadn't realized that Ma was intentionally hiding. As the policeman left down the front steps, she looked back in the direction of her office, still naïvely expecting Ma to emerge with a stack of properly approved temporary residence permits.

In fact Ma didn't emerge until the policeman had long since disappeared. Lin Baihui admonished him: "Where have you been? What about those permits?" "I haven't got them yet," Ma replied. Lin Baihui grew irritated: "Didn't I tell you to sort those out a long time ago? Why haven't you done it?" Ma looked aggrieved but said nothing. He was thinking: *Surely you know I was trying to save you some money!* Lin Baihui guessed what was on his mind and calmed down a bit. Then she recalled how scared he had sounded earlier, and said: "It's no big deal. At least it shouldn't make you quake with terror. Did you think he was going to lock you up or something?" Ma still looked spooked when he replied. "Ms. Lin, you have no idea—he was really fierce!" Lin Baihui asked: "Fierce in what way? He seemed pretty calm to me!" Ma regarded her with suspicion but did not reply. The staff in the diner frequently questioned her judgment, just as she frequently questioned theirs.

Since they were on the topic of residence permits, Ma suddenly asked: "What's the deal with Xu Xingli's younger sister? Should I get a permit for her too? She's not one of our staff, but she's here every day." Lin Baihui thought this was very strange: "Hasn't she gone yet?" Now it was Ma's turn to feel strange: "You mean you didn't know?" Ma was a loyal and devoted manager, and he had felt all along it was not appropriate for Erli to be staying in the dormitory, but Xu Xingli had skillfully managed to give the impression that

Lin Baihui had given permission for Erli to be there.

Ma then changed the subject back to the policeman's visit and re-emphasized the fact that he was happy to deal with all the internal business of the restaurant, but when it came to external relations, he wasn't up to that. *This must be the reason why he isn't able to go off and run his own restaurant,* Lin Baihui speculated. Deciding to forgive him, she asked: "So who's going to do it then?" Ma suggested: "You could do it, or you could hire a public relations woman." Lin Baihui teased him saying: "In other words, you're expecting me to find you a girlfriend?" Ma couldn't help laughing too.

Seeing that no customers were in the diner, Lin Baihui decided to call a meeting of some of the more intelligent female staff, to ask which one would be willing to deal with external relations. They all shook their heads, saying they couldn't do it, and she should hire a local Beijing resident instead. They got to talking about the policeman's visit just before, and their shocked tone was no different from Ma's: it was like the policeman was some kind of terrorist. One girl even recounted with a pale expression: "He was about to take out his handcuffs and drag Manager Ma off to jail!" Lin Baihui refused to believe this. She asked them to describe what the handcuffs looked like, and when they couldn't give a coherent answer, she assumed they were getting worked up into a frenzy and letting their overactive imaginations run wild.

So Lin Baihui put this matter aside for the moment. That day she had got up really early to go and make some purchases in Yuege Village, but Ma had called her before she even got there, and she had to come rushing back. Even though the lunch-hour rush was coming up, she was just too exhausted to deal with it. Partly she was sleepy, and partly it was just a kind of lethargy brought on by her depression. So she headed to the dormitory to lie down for a rest. It was the busiest time of day in the diner, and all the girls were out front, leaving the dormitory empty. She headed straight for the bed beside the back wall and lay down on the lower bunk.

Letting the mosquito net down, she closed her eyes to meditate and recoup her energy. Before long, she was fast asleep. After an indeterminate amount of time, her sleep was broken by a persistent wobbling and creaking of the bed frame. It seemed to be caused by someone climbing up to or down from the top bunk. Reluctantly Lin Baihui rubbed the sleep from her eyes and drowsily recalled that some of the staff had complained about the poor quality of the dormitory beds. At the time, she had dismissed these complaints, because the beds didn't look any different from those she had slept on when she was at university, but now she realized they were completely justified. The beds were really rickety! She immediately felt irritated again. Running a diner was so frustrating—there were just too many annoying little problems that had to be sorted out. Her feelings of depression welled up more strongly. All she wanted to do was go back to sleep, so she rolled over to face the wall and closed her eyes again. The other person apparently sensed her mood and didn't want to disturb her too much, so she tried making each movement very slight, and left some gaps in between each movement to minimize the wobbling. Unfortunately this had the opposite effect: each time she moved, the bed would shake violently, and then there would be a period of calm as the bed gradually stopped wobbling; but just as Lin Baihui thought it was over and started dropping off to sleep, the next violent wobble would disturb her again. After several repetitions of this, Lin Baihui was wide awake.

Opening her eyes, she saw someone's leg dangling outside the mosquito net. Obviously the person was trying to climb down from the top bunk, but didn't know where to put her foot. Lin Baihui rudely shouted: "Can't you come down more quickly?" At this, the leg moved down hesitantly to rest on the outside of the lower bunk, and then the other leg came down to join the first one. The phrase "she's come down" suddenly flashed through Lin Baihui's head. Finally the person was standing on the ground, and of course it turned out to be Erli.

By the time Lin Baihui got up, the lunch hour rush was almost over. She berated herself for being so lazy. She was like that: she would blame herself whenever something like this happened, but the next time she got tired or sleepy, she still couldn't resist the temptation of sleep. Today it was clear when she emerged from the dormitory that she was in a black mood, but the staff didn't know who she was angry with, so they did their best to stay out of her way.

Looking for someone to pick on, Lin Baihui scanned the diner. There was nothing much to see inside the empty dining room, but outside the window she noticed a solid looking man standing outside with his arms folded, looking into the diner.

She recognized him as the boss of the neighboring restaurant, and when he realized he had caught her eye, he gestured for her to come outside. Wondering what he wanted, Lin Baihui went out. Grinning stupidly, he came over to greet her: "Ms. Lin. I see your business is thriving!" "Could be worse," Lin Baihui replied.

As he stood there in front of her, Lin Baihui thought

this guy looked just like you'd expect a restaurant manager to look like in the movies: broad faced with big ears, hair closely shaved, and a stocky, well-built figure. He didn't seem to spend much time managing his own business, but maybe that's because he had a special talent for making difficult things look easy. In fact, his favorite habit seemed to be visiting other peoples' restaurants. Once, not long after Lin Baihui had started her diner, he had eaten three meals there in one day. He also had a tendency to make sardonic little critiques. Like once when he saw a fly in Lin Baihui's diner, he shouted: "Quick, Ms. Lin, get me your fly-swatter and let me have a crack at him!" Looked at objectively, Lin Baihui should have welcomed such constructive criticism, as it could help to improve her business, but even though she made sure to correct the problems he pointed out, she felt resentful of his interference. Doubtless this was just the weakness of human nature.

So this time, after returning his greeting, she wondered to herself uneasily: *What defect is he going to complain about this time?* He asked pompously, "Are you serious about running your business, or is your diner just a way to avoid getting bored at home?" Lin Baihui replied: "Yes, I'm doing it because I can't stand sitting around at home, but no one wants to lose money, right?" He continued: "If you really want to make a profit, you have to spend the whole day here. You can't just turn up for ten minutes here and there. You have no idea what crazy things are going on behind your back." Lin Baihui was reminded of her recent lunch hour nap, and couldn't help blushing as she asked: "What are you talking about?" Her neighbor pursed his lips and whistled: "Aiya! You really don't know. It's totally inappropriate!" Lin Baihui got impatient: "Look, just tell me what happened!"

Finally he got to the point: "Every day some little tramp dressed in her weird country-girl-goes-to-town get up is standing outside your door. It's just not right! The anti-prostitution squad'll be round your place any day now, no doubt about it."

Lin Baihui now realized he was talking about Erli, and her irritation returned, but she refused to accept his insinuations: "So what if she was standing outside the door? That's got nothing to do with prostitution! And I don't have any back rooms for that kind of thing anyway." *You're the one who has back rooms and several pretty girls sitting there all day long with nothing to do but stare out the window. Who knows what kind of funny business they're up to!* she thought to herself.

Hearing Lin Baihui defend herself like this, her neighbor was delighted: "Ah, so you knew about her! I thought she looked so indecent, it must have been someone else arranging it behind your back. I heard you used to be a teacher, but I didn't think you cultured people would be into this sort of thing, eh!" Lin Baihui was left rolling her eyes, furious that he would waste her time with his smutty nonsense.

Turning away, she glanced up at the diner and saw Xu Xingli looking out the window holding a cloth. When Lin Baihui pushed the door open and went in, Xu Xingli came up and greeted her. The neighboring boss was still standing outside laughing and looking at them. Lin Baihui said: "You'd better find your sister a job as soon as possible." Xu Xingli put on a helpless face and pleaded: "Ms. Lin, please let her work at your other location. She'll be happy to do anything: wash dishes, sweep the floor, you name it." Lin Baihui replied: "I thought I already told you, there aren't any vacancies at the other location." She pointed at the guy standing outside and said: "Tell your sister to try next door. It's not far from here and you'll be able to look after each other." When the man saw Lin Baihui pointing at him, he gave a theatrical bow then waved goodbye and sauntered off. As she watched him go, Xu Xingli shook her head: "He's no good. I asked around and found out he hasn't paid his staff for the last half year."

"Could that be true?" Lin Baihui thought. *I wouldn't have guessed a guy like him would have the nerve to do that!*

Xu Xingli continued pleading: "Ms. Lin, I know you're a good sort. My sister's a bit weird and her brain doesn't spin too quick either. I just don't think she'll be safe if we send her anywhere else."

Lin Baihui had noticed quite early on that Xu Xingli was extremely determined. Once she set her mind on a course of action, wild horses couldn't stop her from seeing it through to the end. Despite being given the run around for so long, she hadn't wavered in the least from her original plan to find her sister a job at one of Lin's diners. Lin Baihui couldn't help feeling irritated about being manipulated by an employee, but at the same time the flattery was causing her to waver. Xu Xingli had identified her good point: she never failed to pay her staff's wages. There was nothing special about that really. But Xu Xingli made it sound as if it was something wonderful, and this in turn made it seem more difficult to refuse her request.

Lin Baihui replied: "Okay, okay. But you do know my other diner is in Daxing?" She wanted to emphasize to Xu Xingli that the other location was quite far away, in South Beijing, and it wouldn't be easy to look after her sister once she went there. But Xu Xingli seemed unconcerned: "That don't matter, so long as it's still part of Beijing!"

That same evening, Lin Baihui drove Erli over to her other diner in Daxing.

Soon after dealing with Erli, Lin Baihui decided to hire a laid-off former state enterprise worker in her forties. She wasn't well educated and her language was often laced with profanities, but on the plus side she was completely fearless. Lin Baihui asked her: "If the police came, would you dare to meet them?" Her response: "Why wouldn't I dare to? I dealt with them when I applied for my residence permit." Lin Baihui also asked: "If the disease prevention officer pays us a visit, would you be able to deal with her?" She again replied: "Who hasn't seen the disease prevention officer? My uncle sells disinfectant cabinets to them." Lin Baihui didn't care that her answers made little sense; her brash self-confidence alone was sufficient reason to hire her.

But of course there weren't that many residence permits and external relationships to keep this woman busy full time, so when she wasn't doing those things, Lin Baihui got her to help with simple tasks like washing dishes. Still, Lin Baihui decided to fix her basic salary at fifty yuan per month higher than the other regular staff members like Xu Xingli. When they found out, they unanimously expressed their objections; even Ma clearly thought it was a bad idea. Lin Baihui told them frankly: "I have to apply for temporary residence and work permits for all you non-locals: that costs me five hundred yuan per year per person. She's from Beijing, so she doesn't need any permits. I'm just giving her the money I saved from the permit fees. Isn't that perfectly reasonable?" But the employees still felt aggrieved, and expressed their resentment by giving this new woman the most tiring jobs to do. She, in turn, wasn't about to take any grief from them, and arguments frequently erupted. At first, she tried to mollify them, saying: "It's not my fault I'm from Beijing: I was just lucky enough to inherit my parents' blessings." But it escalated to the point where she would just tell them to "piss off back to where you came from," just like unemployed white Americans sometimes curse the blacks and the Mexicans for supposedly taking their jobs. Once she started swearing at other employees, Ma put on his most solemn expression and sacked her. Lin Baihui couldn't very well stop him, because she had included a clear provision in the Rules of the Diner that swearing was prohibited.

If nothing else, this incident reminded Lin Baihui that she still needed to draft a new rule prohibiting outsiders from staying in the dormitory. Now that Erli was gone, it was the perfect time to ask Ma to add this rule. Ma was willing to make the change, but he objected to the use of the term "outsiders," as he thought it was too easy to associate it with the phrase "people from outside Beijing." So he redrafted the new rule to read: "Absolutely no guests are permitted to stay in the staff dormitory, whether Beijing residents or non-Beijing residents." Lin Baihui didn't bother correcting him. She was willing to allow him a bit of autonomy as long as the basic meaning was clear. Besides, the Rules of the Diner were aimed at the staff, and Ma's version probably made a lot more sense to them than anything she could have written.

The days went by and the diner's business performance indicators went up and down in seemingly random fashion. But in the process, Lin Baihui learned a great deal from Ma about how to run a business. For instance, whenever she wanted to make an announcement to the staff, Lin Baihui would normally photocopy the notice and give each employee an individual copy. This was what she had always done in other organizations where she had worked, and no one had ever questioned it. But Ma told her this was completely unnecessary. What he did was simply post the notice up on the diner's bulletin board and tell all the employees to copy it by hand. The reason he gave was that these employees were all pretty thick, and they wouldn't remember anything unless they had to copy the whole thing out in their own writing. If you just distributed a photocopy to them, they wouldn't even make the effort to read it. Lin Baihui didn't believe him at first, but she realized it was true when she saw several staff members using copies of her latest important announcement as garbage wrappers for their melon seed husks. After adopting Ma's approach, she regularly saw groups of employees clustered in the badly lit corridor copying things down from the bulletin board into their notebooks. They would look up at the board for a few seconds then laboriously write down the characters. Some of them would even use their fingers to guide their reading and make sure they didn't miss any lines. Lin Baihui thought, *What a waste of effort!* But it gave her renewed respect for Ma's real world experience.

Lin Baihui and Ma constantly reversed their roles. For example, it was Ma who had to remind Lin: "You need to be more careful spending money." Lin Baihui was grateful to Ma for noticing this, and she made a point of investigating the diner's expenditures thoroughly, looking for places where cuts could be made. It was only when she started thinking about reducing expenditures that she realized just how much money was flowing out of the diner.

She was thinking about this one day in her office when a middle-aged man walked in unannounced. He introduced himself as an officer from the local neighborhood committee, then fished out his work I.D., his fee collection permit, and a book of invoices, all of which he placed on the table.

Lin Baihui asked: "How can I help you?"

The man, whose name was Li, told her he was there to collect the clean-up fee. Lin Baihui asked him how much it was, and he said it depended on the size of the diner's frontage. He would make some measurements and then multiply the length of Lin Baihui's frontage by the width of the street to obtain the relevant area, and then she would have to pay a hundred yuan per square meter for the clean-up fee.

Hearing his explanation, Lin Baihui finally grasped that the fee was for cleaning the street outside the diner, and she declared: "Well that's the first time I've heard that merchants on both sides of the street have to pay a cleaning fee for the full width of the street." Li replied: "I can show you my fee collector's permit and the official regulation from the Price Bureau giving us the authority to do it."

Since it's based on an official regulation there's not much I can do, Lin Baihui reasoned. She just hoped the final total would not be too high. But the total dollar amount would depend on the result of the measurement. She was very familiar with the length of the diner's frontage, but what about the width of the street? Even though she walked down the street almost every day, she had never thought about measuring it. Her heart was pounding as she wondered, *How wide can it be?*

They went outside together to measure the street. Li took out a tape measure with a metal pin at one end, which he fastened to the base of the curb on the near side of the street. He was extremely meticulous, not the least bit impatient, but this only caused Lin Baihui to stress out even more, as it meant the final total would leave her no room for maneuver, and it might not be to her advantage. Lin Baihui took the other end of the tape measure and after looking both ways to make sure no traffic was coming she crossed the street. With a creaking noise, the tape spooled out behind her like silk from a silk worm. As the tape measure in her hand grew lighter, Lin Baihui's heart grew heavier. Finally she reached the other side and looked at the scale on the tape: fourteen meters! Her head started spinning: she couldn't believe the number she was seeing. Li was still squatting impassively by the other curb, patiently waiting for the facts to speak for themselves. Lin Baihui suddenly had a flash of inspiration: she should squat down too, otherwise with her standing and him squatting the tape was at an angle, and this would make the distance longer. She wanted to minimize it as much as possible. She squatted down, pulled the tape hard to straighten it out, and tried to press the tape onto the edge of the curb, but for some reason it wouldn't straighten out properly. It kept bouncing up and down as if the road was not level. Just then, a pedicab passed in front of Lin Baihui and over the tape measure, crushing the middle part down onto the road. Looking up, Lin Baihui saw it was a street sweeper's pedicab with a long shovel handle sticking out the back. The man riding it called out: "Hi, Department Head Li," and Li nodded without replying, making it look like a truly magnanimous gesture.

After the pedicab passed, the tape bounced back to the height of the curb again, and Lin Baihui was finally able to pull it tight and look at the length. It was twenty centimeters shorter than before, but that wouldn't make any significant difference to the total fee. Lin Baihui stood up, crossing back over the street while making a rapid mental calculation—the annual fee would be four thousand yuan. By the time she crossed the street, Li had reached the same conclusion.

As far as Lin Baihui was concerned, four thousand yuan was far too much. It made her heart ache just to think of it. She decided to challenge it on grounds of unreasonableness. Li took the tape measure back and they went into her office, had fresh cups of tea poured, and began a new round of negotiations.

Li was fully expecting Lin Baihui to bargain. He had a clear sense that this amount was too high, and that no merchant would willingly pay that much, so bargaining was unavoidable. But as soon as Lin Baihui sat down, she exclaimed: "This fee is unreasonable: I can't pay it!" Li found this somewhat annoying. He had already prepared some discount options. For example, he might have said: I'll just ask you to pay for cleaning your side of the street, in other words divide the total by two, and that will save you two thousand yuan. But by absolutely rejecting the reasonableness of the fee, Lin Baihui didn't leave him any room to make a starting offer. So he asked: "If you knew it was unreasonable in the first place, then why waste so much energy measuring the street?"

True enough, thought Lin Baihui. But she tried to justify herself: "I measured the street just now only to find out exactly how much the fee would be. If it had been a small amount, I would have paid it even though it was still unreasonable, but as it is so much, I can't pay."

Li responded: "Exactly: that means there's room for us to negotiate, isn't there?"

Lin Baihui was inexperienced. She didn't grasp that Li was expecting her to bargain the price down. In any case, four thousand yuan was too high to start with; even with a ninety percent discount it would be four hundred yuan, which Lin Baihui was still reluctant to pay. So she continued to insist that the fee was fundamentally wrong: "I can't pay it! Previously the street cleaning was always done by the city environment and sanitation department. When did it suddenly become the job of the neighborhood committee?"

Li explained: "You really think our neighborhood committee wanted to get involved in this pesky business? We're only doing it because the environment and sanitation department refused to." Lin Baihui asked: "Why did they refuse? I'll go and tell them to get their act together!" Li then let the real reason slip out: "It's because this is a newly developed block, and the developer still hasn't made its final payment to the city—that's why the environment and sanitation department won't provide the services." This gave Lin Baihui something else to work with: "So it's like that, is it? In that case, all I need to do is sue the developer. You just wait—I'll get them to pay the money!" By this time, Li was running out of patience. He rejected this proposal out of hand: "Look, I just heard that through the grapevine. It may not even be true." It was obvious he didn't want to make it clear who was really responsible.

Lin Baihui then summed up the situation: "I don't care if it's true or not, you've already explained what the issue is really about. The street cleaning is a burden that's been foisted on the neighborhood committee, and you'd prefer not to do it. In fact you're losing money on it. So on your behalf I'll go and raise a stink about it, and you can wait for me to sort things out, okay?"

Li was now feeling a bit dazed by Lin Baihui's verbal diarrhea, but he managed to latch on to the words "losing money," and declared: "That's true, we are definitely losing money. No matter who we recruit, the minimum we have to pay is several hundred thousand a year. You saw that pedicab man who went over the tape just now? He's one of the guys we hired to clean the streets. Even if you just count their salaries plus food and accommodation, it adds up to well over a hundred thousand a year."

Lin Baihui should have just quietly listened to him rattling on, but she couldn't help testing her wits against him once more: "I know that man. His daughter works in my diner." Li was startled. One could interpret this remark in two different ways: either she was agreeing with his opinion, or she was saying she knew exactly how much it would cost to hire street sweepers, and it wouldn't even come close to a hundred thousand. After coming to his senses, Li decided it must be the latter interpretation, and trying to stay calm he continued: "All our expenditures are properly recorded in the account books, and each year the district government sends someone to do an audit. You don't have the full picture, and of course there are many other expenses that you wouldn't know about."

Lin Baihui said: "Whatever, I can't pay that amount—it's not reasonable." Li had always been accustomed to bargaining, but dealing with people who said it was unreasonable wasn't his strong point. He was feeling quite irritated, and "I'm absolutely not going to discuss with you whether it's reasonable or not" is what he really wanted to say. On the other hand, however, he sensed such bluntness would not be appropriate. Probably in his fee-collecting career, he had never met anyone as tricky to deal with as Lin Baihui. Getting really frustrated, he was on the verge of losing his professional civil servant veneer and taking things much too personally. His eyes narrowed, and with a contemptuous sneer, he said: "Let's face it: the main reason is that you're not making any money."

Hearing this, Lin Baihui felt uncomfortable because it was so true. She was a vain person, a characteristic she probably shared with most business people, but now she was being asked to suppress her vanity. If it had been a smaller amount, vanity might have won through, but four thousand yuan was just too much. She forced herself to smile as naturally as she could, and replied: "You're exactly right. I could possibly manage one or two hundred, but four thousand is completely beyond my means."

Lin Baihui had put aside her vanity to cry poverty once before. The tactic had failed miserably. The previous year one of the waitresses had been rude to a customer, and that led to a big shouting match. The customer turned out to be one of those jerks who find any excuse to extort money, and he demanded five hundred yuan in "compensation." Lin Baihui repeatedly explained that the diner didn't have that kind of money, that the business was actually losing money. But the customer brushed that off with a quite logical response: "It's no concern of mine whether you're making money or losing it. Either way, you offended me, so you have to pay up!"

So this time Lin Baihui waited with baited breath to hear Li's response. Would he say the same thing and demand the full amount?

Surprisingly, Li didn't say anything. In fact he smiled, as if he was happy to hear that Lin Baihui didn't have any money. She took the opportunity to gain a bit more ground by complaining how her costs were increasing, management was incompetent, profit margins were too thin, and so on, until Li grinned and said: "Don't worry, we can take that into account. All we Beijingers need is a reason to start talking!"

It was then that Lin Baihui finally had her great insight: there really are some benefits to being a Beijinger.

After this incident, Lin Baihui changed the way she did things. She no longer tried so hard to justify things based on whether they were reasonable or not. Previously she thought she enjoyed thinking about issues and making rational arguments, but after the cleaning fee incident, she discovered her primary motivation was not reason but self-interest. Up to now, even though you could say she was a kind of business entrepreneur, her motives had been confused. And there were many others like her who dived into the sea of commerce with mixed motives. It was like the start of a marathon: a huge mass of all sorts of people would line up to race, some of them trying a new life experience out of curiosity, some wanting to test their endurance, and still others just hoping to get their photo taken along the route. As they all ran along, the ones with impure motives would fall by the wayside and be disqualified. Only those with the sole motive of winning would be able to stay in the race to the end. Lin Baihui had now joined the handful of competitors left in the business race: people whose only motive was to make lots of money.

After Lin Baihui had purified her motives, most of her former defects automatically disappeared. For example, if she read the newspaper she wouldn't take any notice of superficial stories, but would focus only on the business and finance pages. As for correcting her employees' speech habits, she still did that, but it was for purely practical reasons, not as an outlet for her personal frustrations. And she changed her attitude toward her customers: she displayed spring-like warmth to those whose primary purpose was eating, but frosty and wintry coldness to those who just sat there taking up space and chatting.

The street cleaning fee incident didn't just go away. It resurfaced one day when Ma told Lin Baihui: "Did you know the three biggest restaurants on this street all refused to pay the street cleaning fee, but all the smaller restaurants paid up." Ma put it down to the fact that the bosses of the three biggest restaurants were all native Beijingers, and the people collecting the money didn't dare to bully Beijingers. Lin Baihui could not accept this viewpoint. Her interpretation was that the larger restaurants had wider frontages, so their fees were correspondingly higher, which inevitably meant that they would raise a challenge, and they would have greater justification for it. Ma refused to alter his view, and Lin Baihui guessed he had an inferiority complex. In the past, he had tried running his own restaurant and failed, but instead of learning from the experience, he liked to blame his failure on the fact that he wasn't from Beijing. *Hey,* she thought, *everyone has some knots inside that they can't untie.*

She wanted to point this out to Ma, but she had changed now. She was no longer interested in pointing out the deep inner causes and logic of things. Quite the contrary, now she frequently went along with the wrongheaded ideas of other people. On this occasion, she just put on an indignant face and attacked the household registration system. She told Ma that the household registration system was one of the key reasons why Chinese society was unfair. What right did they have to say that only people born in Beijing could have a Beijing residence permit? People in America didn't have to put up with such a system.

Lin Baihui had been to America, and sometimes during a conversation she would make references to what it was like in America. On this occasion, Ma asked in surprise: "You're saying America doesn't have a household registration system?" "Of course they don't," Lin Baihui said. "It's only money that counts in America. If you can find a job in New York and afford to buy a New York house, then you are a New York resident and your children can go to school in New York." After saying this, she brought the topic round to Ma again, trying to buck up his spirits: "You've done great things in Beijing, and our diner is a place for you to develop your talents to their full potential. You should just ignore those snobby people. As long as you keep on working hard, the time will surely come when you can buy both a house and a car in Beijing."

Ma felt a lot better after that and said he would keep working hard for the diner, and he capped it off by immediately making several reasonable proposals for improving the diner's performance.

A few days later, another man suddenly turned up at the diner. He introduced himself as Mr. Xue from the neighborhood committee.[1] Lin Baihui asked: "How can I help you?" He replied: "I had lunch here yesterday. I was sitting at the same table as Department Head Liu." Lin Baihui said: "That's great. Are you here for lunch again today?" But he replied: "I was sitting next to Department Head Liu, and I saw you give him his money back!"

Department Head Liu was responsible for fines and penalties, so Lin Baihui never dared to charge him for meals

---

1. In the original Chinese, Wang gives this character the surname 胥, which is written as Xu in pinyin. It is a different character from the surname of Xu Xingli and her family, which is 许, so Chinese readers would immediately see the difference, but the pinyin spelling is the same. To avoid confusion from here on, we have slightly altered this character's surname to Xue.

when he came, but that day the waitress didn't recognize him and carelessly asked him to pay. Department Head Liu was very reasonable about it and paid up without a complaint, but when Lin Baihui came in and saw him sitting there, she immediately went over and gave him his money back.

Lin Baihui was shocked when this Mr. Xue brought the incident up again. At first she thought he must be from the anti-corruption squad. But then she reasoned: there's nothing wrong with giving somebody a discount. If he starts raising a stink about it, I'll just say: well that was an amazing coincidence, wasn't it! Department Head Liu just happened to be our ten thousandth customer, and we decided to give him a special reward of a free meal.

But in fact Xue hadn't anything to do with the anti-corruption squad. He was just making conversation to break the ice. Actually he was from the building department, in charge of collecting the street cleaning fee. Lin Baihui immediately thought of old Li and asked: "So you must know Department Head Li then?" Mr. Xue replied: "Yes, I know him: he's my deputy. I never get directly involved in the fee collection. I leave it all to him." Lin Baihui said: "So in other words, *you're* the real department head!" He laughed and replied: "All that department head nonsense. It just means more things to worry about!"

Lin Baihui waited for him to get to the point, trying to keep a polite smile on her face. He continued: "Actually there's something I need to ask you. I hope it's not too much trouble?"

His tone made it clear that this was nothing to do with the street cleaning fee, so Lin Baihui replied: "No problem. Tell me what you need."

It was actually very simple. On the neighborhood

committee, Mr. Xue was in charge of keeping the streets tidy, and one of his street cleaners was from the countryside, and his daughter had just arrived in Beijing and was looking for work. When Mr. Xue came to eat at the diner yesterday, the director of the neighborhood committee was there too, and he said he was looking for a live-in nanny. A couple of weeks earlier he had seen a young girl from the countryside standing outside this diner. When Xue made some enquiries, he found out the girl was the younger daughter of his street cleaner, but she had recently been sent to work at the Daxing Diner, which Lin Baihui also owned.

Lin Baihui said: "You must be talking about Erli."

Department Head Xue replied: "Our director was very impressed by her, so I wanted to discuss with you the possibility of letting her go and work at the director's house."

Lin Baihui said: "As far as I'm concerned that's no problem at all. To tell you the truth, we have too many people working at that location. I only gave her the job as a favor to her sister, and to stop her standing outside here making an exhibition of herself."

Department Head Xue said: "We'll pay you an appropriate amount, of course."

Lin Baihui replied: "You don't need to pay me anything. She's not like a professional football player with a transfer fee attached!" Department Head Xue didn't seem to get this joke—he obviously didn't have a sense of humor—so she kept things businesslike: "If you can just ask her father to write a note to his daughter telling her about the new job, I'll drive over to Daxing and show it to her, and then bring her back here."

Department Head Xue hadn't expected the problem to be solved so easily, and his face was immediately wreathed in smiles: "That's excellent! I'll tell her father to come here straightaway."

Soon that middle-aged man with the familiar high protruding cheekbones walked up to the diner. Lin Baihui was sitting in the middle of the dining room, and Xu Xingli was wiping down the bar area. The man hesitated at the door, not sure whether he should go in, and it was Xu Xingli who broke the silence. She put down her cloth and went to greet her father.

Lin Baihui thought Xu Xingli hadn't heard about this business, but observing her expression now, it was obvious she knew everything. She doubtless would have preferred to pretend she was not involved, but her father's timidity gave her no choice but to show her hand.

Xu Xingli led her father over to where Lin Baihui was sitting. Lin Baihui took a good look at him. He was definitely the guy she had collided with while driving the other week. She nodded at him politely, but inside she felt like laughing. With father and daughter both standing in front of her, it was so obvious how the genes had been passed down from one to the other. Their distinctive feature was the protruding cheekbones, but having said that, the cheekbones had quite a different impact depending on which face you looked at. The father was short and skinny, so his cheekbones stuck out so far he looked like a cartoon character. People would have a natural tendency to scorn a middle-aged cartoon character, but on top of this the skin on his face and hands was rough and dirty, and the rest of his body was covered in a gingery brown costume that was doubtless his work uniform. This wrinkled, old-fashioned, ridiculous cartoon character covered with dust stood before Lin Baihui looking insignificant and completely lacking in authority.

By comparison, his daughter seemed much more impressive. She was wearing the diner's standard-issue uniform, but accessorized with her own two-inch-thick platform shoes. She was actually very slim, apart from her prominent cheeks which made her face look fatter than she really was, and as she stood there in those dictionary-thick platform soles, she seemed much more substantial than her father. As Lin Baihui was seated, Xu Xingli's head was above her, which helped to reduce the impact of the cheeks and keep them in proportion with the rest of her body. Somehow this made her seem more sincere.

Xu Xingli started by apologizing to Lin Baihui: "Ms. Lin, I'm really sorry my sister's leaving Daxing so soon." Lin Baihui was actually quite delighted, because she really didn't want Erli working there, and this was the perfect excuse to let her go, like a free gift she never expected. She had been feeling very satisfied with the whole situation, but somehow Xu Xingli's apology made her feel she'd been cheated. She pulled a long face, and replied: "Well exactly. And who was it that insisted so strongly on sending Erli there in the first place?"

Old Mr. Xu tried to explain: "I thought that kind of servant's work was not right for her, but when the neighborhood committee director said he wanted to hire her, I didn't dare say no, you understand?"

"I don't really buy that. It's more a case of if you can make your director happy, he's more likely to give you a few more street cleaning contracts."

Old Xu looked embarrassed: "I won't lie to you: I was hoping for that too."

Xu Xingli glared at her father. Seeing her expression, for some reason Lin Baihui suddenly sensed that this job move was not really in Erli's interests. She started to worry that Erli might refuse to come back with her, so she reminded Erli's dad: "Why don't you write a note for your daughter."

He asked: "What do you think I should write?"

Lin Baihui replied: "Just write what you want to say, of course!"

"What is it that I want to say?"

Xu Xingli interrupted impatiently: "Look, just write this, Dad: 'Erli, I've found you another job. After you read this note, come back with Ms. Lin,'"

Her dad looked worried: "Why don't you write it then?"

But Lin Baihui strongly objected to this: "No, it has to be your dad who writes it."

Looking disgruntled, Xu Xingli said, "In that case, Ms. Lin, I'll get back to work." Lin Baihui replied, "Good idea." Xu Xingli then strutted off stiffly in her two-inch heels, leaving her dusty haired and grimy faced cartoon of a father staring blankly at the paper and pen in front of him.: *No matter what you say, he is still the father, and he has to do it,* Lin Baihui thought.

Finally he wrote out the note, although Lin Baihui had to wait patiently as he wrote the first draft and then replaced it with a second draft. In the second draft, he intentionally changed a few characters to running script. The result was that his regular characters looked like bundles of split firewood propped up unsteadily on the ground, but in between them were squeezed several smooth, writhing snakes. As Lin Baihui took the note from him, she thought: *People must think this guy is quite cultivated back in his home village!*

When Old Xu saw Lin Baihui taking the note, he thanked her profusely. It was all she could do to stop him from bowing down before her. She couldn't help feeling self-satisfied: such a small amount of effort on her part to earn such deep gratitude was a worthwhile use of resources.

Lin Baihui made sure everything was shipshape in the diner, then walked outside. It was that time of year when it keeps fluctuating between warm and cold, and a sudden gust of wind hit her, causing her to bend forward. After the wind died down, she found her shiny car was now covered with a layer of dust. She wasn't really concerned about the car being dirty, but it had covered the windshield too, which affected her visibility. She had to return to the diner to get a cloth and wipe it off.

Just as she was wiping the windshield, Old Xu came back and spotting Lin Baihui exclaimed: "Well thank the heavens above you haven't left yet!"

"Did you forget something?"

"Yes, I forgot to ask you: if Erli can't cope with the job at the director's place, you'll still take her back to Daxing, won't you?"

"What are you talking about?" Lin Baihui stopped wiping the windshield for a moment.

Old Xu repeated: "What I'm saying is: if the director's job turns out to be no good, you'll take Erli back, won't you?"

"Where on earth did you get that idea?"

Old Xu looked shocked. "You mean you won't do it?"

"Just think about what you're saying. After Erli leaves, I'll have to hire someone else, but then if Erli's not satisfied with her job at the director's house, and she wants to go back to Daxing, I'll have to see whether I'm satisfied with the new girl or not. If I'm not satisfied, then I might consider hiring Erli back; but if I *am* satisfied, then there won't be any place left for Erli. It's first come, first served in this business." In fact, Lin Baihui was certain that once Erli left, she would

157

have a full complement of staff at the other location, and there would be no need to hire anyone at all, let alone take Erli back.

Old Xu stared blankly at Lin Baihui. Probably her explanation contained too many conditional clauses and he hadn't managed to completely process it yet. Lin Baihui turned back to continue wiping the windshield while she waited for his response, but even after quite some time he said nothing. When she looked around again, he was already gone.

After she finished wiping the glass, she sat in the car ready to start the engine, but then she found the windshield wasn't clean at all. There were still brown streaks across it which she hadn't seen from outside. Her cloth was already dirty, so she had to go and get a clean one from the diner. As she came out of the kitchen into the dining room, she found that Old Xu was back outside again. Probably he thought she was sitting in the car, and he was peering in with his face pressed on the car window. Finding no one inside, he straightened up and headed toward the diner. Both his protruding cheeks now had muddy marks on them.

Lin Baihui thought: *Even the people hired to clean the streets have so much free time; it would be much better for me to look for a job in a state enterprise!* Subconsciously she guessed that he was about to make things even more complicated. But some devilish impulse caused her to head over to the bar and pick up the telephone. By then, Old Xu had reached the glass door of the diner and was looking in. Seeing Lin Baihui on the phone, he stood outside trying to be tactful. For reasons that weren't even clear to herself, Lin Baihui dialed the number of Department Head Xue, and notified him that things had all been arranged and Erli would go to the director's house that evening. While talking she was wondering why this call was even necessary. Whether Erli actually went to the director's house was none of her business; it was really just a matter of Erli resigning one job and starting another one. Why was she making such a big deal about it?

Department Head Xue was clearly delighted though, and he kept repeating polite remarks like "sorry to put you to so much trouble." Lin Baihui still wasn't completely sure of her motives, but it seemed to be mainly that she needed to hear these words of gratitude. She should have politely demurred, but in her muddle-headed state, she forgot to.

Hanging up the phone, she headed to the door where Old Xu was patiently waiting. As soon as he saw her coming out, he went up to her and abruptly declared: "I've changed my mind. I want Erli to stay in Daxing."

Lin Baihui asked why.

"I went to the director's house myself to make enquiries. That job is no good: she won't be able to manage. There's a two-year-old toddler and an eighty-year-old granny to look after."

"If they didn't have people who needed looking after, then why would they hire a nanny?"

"Our Erli is only seventeen. She can't do that kind of work."

"Working in a diner is really tiring too."

The old man replied: "I know, but Erli isn't afraid of hard work. She just can't stand being picked on by other people."

Lin Baihui grew irritated. "So why didn't you go there earlier to find out the situation? It's a bit late to go now, after you've agreed to let her do it."

"I thought if she couldn't manage it she could always

return to your diner. How was I supposed to know that once she left you wouldn't take her back?" Old Xu replied.

At that instant, Lin Baihui suddenly understood everything with great clarity. She had assumed that all those words of gratitude earlier were effectively a free gift to her. But in fact, Old Xu's gratitude was because he had wrongly assumed that she would take Erli back. And Department Head Xue's gratitude was because he too thought she had agreed to this irrational demand. This was not a case of an employee resigning to take another job; it was sheer bullying.

But how could they possibly have thought she would take Erli back? When had she ever made any such promise?

Lin Baihui frowned and searched her memory until she recalled that Department Head Xue had indeed said something along those lines. When Lin Baihui had told him the joke about "football transfers" and not needing to be paid for this "transaction," Department Head Xue had said: "We'll have to see how both sides get along with one another. If they can't come to an agreement, then she will have to go back."

It was just typical of Lin Baihui to have ignored this remark. She slapped herself on the forehead, and exclaimed: "I'm really getting senile!" It was not the first time she had made such a mistake. She constantly neglected those elements of reality that didn't fit with what she wanted. She edited the facts to suit her version of the truth. But life was not as simple as that, and the elements she had neglected were still buried in her subconscious mind ready to be released again when the conditions were right, and to recreate the complete picture of reality once more. Her recurring depression was largely caused by these frequent mistakes and belated corrections. She thought, *If I really were old I could be*

completely obstinate and refuse to admit any of my mistakes.
But in my current senile-but-still-young state, it's just painful.
She then transferred her self-censure to a different topic. She deeply regretted having told Erli's father that she wouldn't let Erli come back to Daxing. She shouldn't have said anything. If she had just brought Erli over and dumped her on her father's lap, it would have been too late for them to say anything. *Damn! I'm so dense!* she cursed to herself. "Why did I have to go mouthing off just then!" Thinking about it, she concluded it was because she had been carried away by her self-confidence, her delight that she had finally rid herself of the Erli problem. And the reason she had been so self-confident was that she had Old Xu's note in her hand. Who could have guessed he would change his mind after he wrote that note?

She tried a final challenge: "But you already wrote a note."

The old man didn't seem too concerned: "Yes, I wrote a note, and that's why I came back to find you, and ask you not to give the note to Erli. That will solve the problem won't it?"

"But you already wrote it."

"Just don't give it to her, okay?"

He looked at Lin Baihui earnestly, believing that his demand was perfectly reasonable. Lin Baihui could only curse to herself: *Damn my stupid superstition about the power of language! I thought having a note in my hand meant his daughter would definitely go.* Seeing she did not respond, the old man seemed to guess what she was thinking, and boldly suggested: "What's the big deal? I'll write another note." Saying this, he rapidly scrawled something on a piece of paper and gave it to Lin Baihui. It said: "Erli, keep working

161

hard at Daxing."

As Lin Baihui drove along, fine flakes of snow were starting to fall. Despite the fact that Old Xu had written his retraction note, Lin Baihui was determined to bring Erli back from Daxing. The only thing she couldn't think of right now was an appropriate excuse. Since the father had withdrawn his consent, she would have to do things in a rational way, totally by the book. She couldn't just go storming in to the Daxing diner and shout: "Erli, you're fired, and don't ask me why!"

All the way there, she tried to think up a suitable excuse. Even though she could be quite calculating at times, and it should have taken her only a few minutes to think up a plan, somehow she found it difficult this time. Deep inside, she felt she was doing something wrong, but then again she couldn't quite put her finger on it. It was very cold outside and the car windows were misted up, making it hard for Lin Baihui get a clear view. She had to turn on the air conditioning to de-mist the windows. This certainly cleared the windshield but soon she was shivering with cold, so she turned it off again. Then of course the mist stubbornly returned. Lin Baihui was hesitating about whether to turn on the air-conditioning again when suddenly the brake lights of the car in front glowed red and she had to slam on her brakes. The road was slippery in the snowy conditions, which meant her car took longer to come to a halt than normal. Seeing the car in front getting closer and closer, Lin Baihui broke out in a cold sweat.

Fortunately, just when she thought her car was going to crash, the car in front abruptly moved off again. Lin Baihui exhaled heavily and thought: *What the hell is wrong with me?*

She couldn't work out what was wrong with her because she had already buried her capacity for self-reflection and rational thought. She used to have that capacity, even if she wasn't good at it, but it was at least there. It was like a large Chinese-manufactured industrial machine, not very refined but operating more or less reliably. The workers would say of it: "Look, at least we have our own machinery." But now this piece of machinery had been completely abandoned and left to rust.

And yet, on the other hand, even just having a factory building containing an abandoned rusty machine was better than a completely empty building. Though Lin Baihui could no longer think properly, she could still feel things, and what she felt was something in the back of her throat preventing her from breathing properly. She was also yawning a lot, which was a sign of a lack of oxygen. After breathing in a few times to increase her oxygen intake, her eyes started watering and became misty, just like the windows of the car.

Behind this mist she could vaguely make out an image of Erli, though she only knew it was Erli because of the protruding cheekbones appearing and disappearing in the fog. This distinctive image reminded Lin Baihui that she was on her way to meet someone. She mouthed the words "Erli, Erli" several times, and as she mumbled the name she kept picturing those pointy cheekbones.

Eventually, only the name remained and the image of Erli disappeared. When that happened, the name seemed to lose its personal associations and became just an abstract sign, and when it became just a sign Lin Baihui suddenly realized she had a workable strategy.

By the time Lin Baihui drove back to the diner with Erli,

it was already getting dark. She told Xu Xingli to find her father and she sat down in the dining room, exhausted. Erli seemed to have no idea what was going on, but Lin Baihui couldn't be bothered to explain things to her. She remained standing outside. During that time, several customers came in, and some of them recognized Erli and gave her a puzzled look. Erli seemed to feel that this diner was a taboo place, and she should not enter it. That was good: at least it showed there was no link between her and the diner.

After quite some time, Xu Xingli and her father hurried in. Lin Baihui immediately said, "Your daughter doesn't have a proper ID, so I can't keep her in my diners. You'd better tell her to go to the director's house. The police won't dare check peoples' IDs there."

"Of course she doesn't have an ID card—she's not eighteen yet," said Old Xu.

"Not eighteen? Well that's another reason why I can't keep her on."

Old Xu opened his mouth, as if he was about to say: are you really claiming you didn't know Erli was under eighteen? But he said nothing, doubtless realizing that any words would be superfluous.

As the two of them turned and went down the steps, Lin Baihui suddenly remembered something: "Oh, by the way, here are your notes." She fished the two handwritten notes out of her handbag and returned them to Old Xu.

A few days later, Xu Xingli was sitting in the diner crying. Lin Baihui asked her what was wrong, but she said nothing. Lin Baihui guessed it was something to do with Erli. What could have happened? She was curious, but didn't want to ask too directly, and she didn't feel it was really necessary for her to pretend that she really cared. Xu Xingli wasn't willing to talk about it either. She felt awkward because she was the one who had tried to organize everything for her sister—it wasn't really Lin Baihui's fault—and all her vacillating and changing of Erli's job had obviously reduced Lin Baihui's opinion of her.

Gradually Lin Baihui started to understand what was bothering Xu Xingli, and she felt a lot less guilty. One day, when the diner was quieter than usual, she adopted a let's-put-the-cards-on-the-table attitude and drew Xu Xingli aside to ask her how Erli was getting on. After some prodding, Xu Xingli explained that Erli's psychological problems had flared up again and she had already returned to their home village. When Lin Baihui heard this, she couldn't help letting slip a tactless joke: "Ah, so she's 'gone back up' again!" Maybe she was trying to get closer to Xu Xingli by imitating her dialect, but Xu Xingli didn't seem to get it. She just looked silently at Lin Baihui.

Xu Xingli's look gave Lin Baihui a major shock. What did she mean by it? Having stopped reflecting on things a long time ago, Lin Baihui had now become a simple-minded person; it seemed she no longer had the linguistic ability to explain the shock that Erli's look had given her. All she knew was that it made her feel uncomfortable. That look penetrated the fog that had been shrouding her eyes for such a long time and pierced her right in the heart.

✤ ✤ ✤

About the Author and the Translators

Wang Yuan graduated from the Department of Chinese Language and Literature, Peking University, in 1988. She has published four novels, one collection of short stories, and one prose collection. Her works were shortlisted for the prestigious Lu Xun Literary Prize in 1998. Wang Yuan was a contract writer for the Beijing Writers' Association from 2000 to 2005. She currently divides her time between Beijing and Los Angeles.

Colin S. Hawes currently teaches Chinese and corporate law at the University of Technology Sydney, but he has never lost his appetite for literature since completing his Ph.D. in classical Chinese poetry at the University of British Columbia in the late 1990s. Besides translating Wang Yuan's stories, he has completed a cross-cultural comic mystery novel with a Taoist slant and published two academic books on contemporary Chinese corporate culture and Song dynasty poetry.

Shuyu Kong is an associate professor of humanities and director of the Asia-Canada program at Simon Fraser University, Canada. She has lived, studied and worked in China, Canada and Australia and keeps herself busy with bilingual writing and cross-continental traveling. She is the author of *Consuming Literature: Bestsellers and the Commercialization of Literary Production in Contemporary China* (Stanford University Press, 2005), and *Popular Media, Social Emotion and Public Discourse in Contemporary China* (Routledge, 2014).